Sherlock Holmes
and
The Baker Street Dozen

A collection of thirteen short stories

Sherlock Holmes
and
The Baker Street Dozen

A collection of thirteen short stories

Val Andrews

**BREESE
BOOKS
LONDON**

First published in 1997 by
Breese Books Ltd
164 Kensington Park Road, London W11 2ER, England

© Breese Books Ltd, 1997

ISBN: 0 947533 41 9

Typeset in 11½/14pt Caslon by
Ann Buchan (Typesetters), Middlesex
Printed and bound in Great Britain by
Itchen Printers Ltd, Southampton

Contents

The Kinema Mystery

The sounds produced by an arriving client and the tread upon the stairs which followed had long been a source of entertainment for Sherlock Holmes. He would tell what sort of a visitor to expect and more often than not he was accurate. Mr Septimus Gregson proved to be very much as Holmes had predicted as he appeared in the doorway; heavily built, ponderous and smoking a Havana cigar of a brand known as Perfecto. I could understand how the detective had read the message of Gregson's tread but I was amazed that he had been able to detect the exact brand of the cigar after giving his nasal passages such abuse through strong pipe tobacco for so long.

Gregson spoke with the tones of a self-made man; grammatically correct, yet with the trace of a London accent. He shook hands with us both as Holmes made the introductions and said, 'Mr Holmes, Doctor Watson, it is good of you to see me at short notice, but the matter is pressing. I hesitate to use the words urgent or serious because I do not believe there is a risk worse than that of loss of property.'

Holmes indicated a comfortable chair and I draped his greatcoat across a high backed seat. 'Just tell me what it is that troubles you, Mr Gregson, and Watson and I will decide upon its degree of gravity.'

Gregson started to explain, 'I am the owner of three London kinema theatres. You are, I feel sure, familiar with the moving pictures as a form of entertainment?'

I said, 'Holmes and I attended a performance of that remarkable invention at Maskelynes a few years ago.'

Holmes added, 'But I thought that the novelty had worn off and the invention was confined now to demonstrations in fairground booths, empty shops and other fly-by-night entertainments?'

Gregson replied, 'This was true until quite recently but now, as we are moving into the twentieth century, the moving pictures are growing up. I have caused three pur-pose-made kinemas — as I call them — to be built. These have seating to rival that of a music hall with a special silvered screen upon which to project the images. The films, as we call them, are accompanied by a pianist who captures the mood of each scene.

'The aisles are carpeted and there is in each building an attractive entrance lobby with a booking office and stalls for the sale of cigars, cigarettes and confections. I must tell you that my little chain of kinemas has really taken off and other showmen are already trying to copy my methods.'

After a very short pause Holmes said, 'I am delighted to hear of your success, Mr Gregson, but what is the problem that you think I might help you with?'

Gregson said, 'I'll get straight to the point. A week ago my kinema in the Edgware Road had a stock of expensive Havana cigars stolen from the lobby.'

With a vague hint of impatience Holmes said, 'You have informed the police?'

He answered, 'Yes sir, but the crime, minor as it was,

baffled them. You see, the theft must have been committed during the night, after the kinema was closed, yet there was no sign of a forced entry. When the staff arrived in the morning everything was exactly as it should have been, except for the missing cigars. I was myself the last to leave the building to lock it, and the first to arrive to unlock it on the following morning.'

I murmured, 'Let us hope that with forewarning it will never happen to your other enterprises.'

He said, 'That is just the point, doctor, I was willing to write the incident off, puzzling and irritating as it might be but three days later a second of my kinemas was robbed of its cigars. The circumstances were the same as at Edgware Road, with my resident manager experiencing the same thing. Now I fear for the safety of all three buildings. There appears to be some sort of master criminal who can enter and leave my secured premises without leaving any sort of trace. It is not practical to regularly transport the stock of cigars in and out of the buildings. Moreover, their sale is a very useful added source of profit — at least, it was!'

Holmes blew through the mouthpiece of a briar prior to filling it with the black shag which seemed to have been chosen for that day. 'I can see the problem; if no locked premises are safe then your only course is to employ a night watchman.'

Gregson assented but added, 'This would reduce my profits, and yet perhaps be no help.'

I said, 'How can it fail to prevent a repetition?'

He said, 'Because this is no ordinary thief, there is almost a touch of the supernatural in it all.'

Holmes chuckled, 'A ghost of Bill Sykes perhaps? Oh

come, Mr Gregson, we are dealing with a real life crime carried out by a criminal who is very much alive.'

Gregson asked, 'You will help me then?'

Holmes nodded, 'Of course, for it is an enigma worthy of my involvement.' Then he turned to me, 'Watson, send Billy for a hansom, the third on the rank, for we are bound for the Edgware Road.'

Almost opposite the Metropolitan Music Hall we saw the brand new kinema with its rich blue letters on the façade. Holmes examined the locks of the already opened doors at the front entrance. He took his lens to the close scrutiny and mumbled, 'I am not saying that these locks could not be opened other than with the keys, but I feel that some trace or scratch might be left and there is none. In any case this very busy thoroughfare is well patrolled by night. I am more interested in other means of entry. Let us go inside, Gregson.'

We discovered that the only other doors were of the exit variety, opening onto a side alley. These could be opened only from the inside, by means of a pressure bar and Gregson showed us the fearsome-looking bar and padlocks fitted to the exterior at night. Windows, there were few and all of them far too small for a man to pass through. Gregson explained, 'Daylight is unwelcome in a kinema. The windows are solely for ventilation.'

We sat in the front row of the kinema stalls, Holmes glancing keenly around him as if seeking inspiration. The screen filled most of the wall which formed one end of the simple building. At each side of the screen there were velvet draperies, swagged for effect. Behind us, at the entrance end, there was a moving-picture projector standing upon a sturdy base, raised up and with steps for the operator to mount that he might attend the machine.

At length, Holmes rose from his seat and paced around the auditorium. He explained to me, rather as if I was of limited intellect, 'You see, Watson, unlike a theatre proper there is no stage and in consequence no backstage area. No wings, flies or dressing rooms, just a solid wall with a screen attached to it.' I took no offence at his style of comment, knowing from experience that he was simply thinking aloud for his own benefit. As Gregson and I made for the entrance Holmes dallied, and lifted one of the drapes beside the screen. I thought I saw him pick something up and place it in his wallet. When I asked him about this he made light of it. 'Probably nothing of importance, Watson, but if it proves otherwise you will soon know. Tell me, Gregson, do your cleaners do a good job?'

Gregson waved an all-encompassing hand around him, 'Can you see any reason for me to complain of them?'

Holmes had dismissed the cab, so we hailed another which took us to the second of the crime-affected kinemas, this time in a suburb of Finchley. Here we were confronted by an almost identical scenario. The building had obviously been fashioned from the same architectural plans. Again we examined all, and again Holmes dallied to peer beneath one of the drapes at the same side of the screen as the one he had looked under at Edgware Road. This time he evidently found nothing to interest him but, rather as from an afterthought, peered under the drape at the opposite side of the screen. I thought I caught a gasp of satisfaction from him, as he picked up a small object once more.

As we left the kinema we piled into the hansom cab, which Holmes had retained in anticipation of our stay being a shorter one than at the Edgware Road kinema. 'Where is your third and last exhibition venue, Gregson?'

The impresario said, 'Not far from here at Wood Green.' Soon we were in another leafy suburb and confronted by another Gregson kinema of a design now very familiar to us. We made the same investigative round, Holmes even repeating his examination of the floor beneath the drapes at each side of the screen. This time, evidently, he found nothing of interest.

The audience were beginning to arrive and quite soon from the lobby we could hear the tinkling of a piano and a little later the laughter and appreciation of a small but lively audience. We peered in through the curtained door to the auditorium and saw the flickering images of riders straight from the great plains and then those of comedians in police uniforms, falling over each other. Holmes remarked, 'The public, Watson, are easily entertained!'

We sat upon a chesterfield in the lobby and Holmes was particularly thoughtful, 'If there is any pattern in the thief's mind, tonight would be a likely time for this very place to be robbed.' I worked it out in my mind. Seven nights ago the robbery at Edgware Road, three nights later that at Finchley. I had to agree that we were present at a possibly opportune time but, to my extreme disappointment, Holmes bade me return to Baker Street. 'Inform Mrs Hudson that I will not be present for dinner — and Watson, you may not see me for some hours.'

Not until the early hours of the following morning did I see Holmes again but I had not retired for the night, preferring to smoke quietly and doze by the sitting-room fire. Then at about two of the clock there were the sounds of a hansom arriving, and soon Sherlock Holmes stood before me with a gleam of triumph in his eyes.

'Well, Watson, my dear fellow, you can chronicle another case solved by Sherlock Holmes! The sheer ingenuity of it all suddenly struck me like a bolt from the blue. The thief did not need to break in to make the robbery because he was already inside. You see at the conclusion of the performance there is a momentary blackout, before the auditorium lights are raised. He took advantage of that to secrete himself behind a drape at one side of the screen. Then, when all but he had left, he was able, with all the time he needed, to take that which he had come for, a bag full of expensive cigars.'

I could see the ingenuity of this but spotted at once a flaw in the plan. 'How then, pray, did he get out?'

Holmes laughed, 'He did not, at least not until the staff had arrived and opened the building upon the following morning. When he heard them coming he hid himself once more behind his drape, and awaited a suitable moment to make his escape unobserved through the now unsecured side exit into the alley. Probably he took advantage of all persons present being lured to the cigar stall. Anyway, those first two occasions but not this time! I took equal advantage of the blackout to hide behind the screen. Although it hid me I could still see through due to the nature of its making. I waited until he returned with the loot. When I apprehended him, Gregson and the local police came to my prearranged signal; a police whistle.'

I gasped at the ingenuity and yet the simplicity of it all.

Yet one thing still puzzled me. I asked, 'Holmes, what really told you that he hid behind a drape?'

He smiled, 'Well, I could not know for sure until I caught him redhanded, but suspect it, ah, that was another matter. It was only for the sake of being thorough that I glanced under the curtains at Edgware Road. I found this.' He took out his wallet and tipped out a cigarette end. 'Egyptian Pasha, an unusual brand.' He tipped a second cigarette end into his palm. 'This one, also a Pasha, I found under a curtain at Finchley. Had he been there long enough I would have found a third tonight. It is difficult for a regular smoker to be long denied his drug!'

The Strange Case of the Burmese Jungle Fowl

My friend Mr Sherlock Holmes solved many, or most, of his principal cases through the science of deduction allied to his amazing energetic activity. Yet there were other cases often of a less than serious nature which he solved simply through that enormous general knowledge which was stored in his file of a brain, plus his alertness of eye. Just such a case was that of the disappearing jungle fowl.

We came into contact with these exotic birds through Holmes's association with a certain Mr Chapman who had a rather unusual occupation in the importation and trade in exotic creatures from the four corners of the globe. He operated from premises just off the Fleet Street end of the Strand which from the outside looked as unremarkable as the average warehouse, yet from which emanated the sounds produced by a myriad of exotica. Inside Chapman's, of course, the stock of his trade could be clearly seen. Huge cages on wheels housed lions, leopards and bears, whilst an elephant or two could usually be seen, chained and swaying their great grey bodies at the far end of the large building. Between these larger creatures were stationed boxes, baskets and hutches containing smaller examples of his strange trade; snakes, civets, even small crocodilians and glass bells and tanks containing strange fish and amphibians. Above hung cages which housed hawks and eagles as well as the more usual cockatoos and macaws. I need hardly add that the noise within Chapman's was indescribable, with shrieks, snarls and other wild cries, plus those made by the scampering of rats in the deep litter as they were stalked by the owner's domestic cats.

The attraction of this strange London backwater for Sherlock Holmes was not merely that of idle curiosity, for old Chapman had been a source of useful information to the detective when the scientists at the Natural History Museum had failed him. Did I mention, for instance, his useful advice and correct identification of the giant rat of Sumatra?

We were strolling in the Strand following a meal at Simpsons with a client of Holmes's. I believe it was I who suggested a visit to Chapman's with Sherlock quite happy to dally there a while. We entered the building to be by the old livestock dealer himself. He was as stout and ruddy-faced as ever and wearing his usual Fair Isle jersey with twill trousers and buckle boots.

He welcomed us, 'Mr Holmes, Doctor, glad I am to see you. Just let me finish selling Lord George some timber wolves and then my time is yours.' We knew George Sanger of old, no more a nobleman than I.

We exchanged pleasantries as he picked out the three young wolves that he wanted. 'Chapman, I'll give you fifteen pounds for the three and I'll send Alpine Charlie with a shifting den to fetch them.' This Lord of the Ring touched his crop to his silk hat as he departed.

As soon as he was out of earshot Chapman said, 'Great

eye he has got, picks out the best of the bunch every time, but always pays over the odds. Just as well because at present I'm losing a fortune on the Burmese jungle fowl!'

Intriguing as this statement was Holmes seemed inclined to ignore it but curiosity got the best of me. 'Lost a few to fowl pest or bumble foot?'

He shook his head, 'No, that I could accept, for I lose a few of my specimens to disease each season. But these Jungle fowl are vanishing as fast as I can import them. Where are the little blighters going?' He had thrown his cards on the table and politeness alone made the mildly uninterested detective pick them up. Chapman showed us the pen which housed the birds which was perhaps ten feet square with an open top and a small mesh door for access. To me the birds were just chickens, albeit handsome ones with a beautiful gloss to their rusty red plumage.

I asked, 'Who buys them from you?'

Chapman replied, 'Noblemen mostly, them as has stately homes where they like them around in the grounds. None of your common-or-garden Buff Orpingtons for the likes of they.'

Holmes took the bait, 'You see, Watson, these are the original fowl from which the domestic variety has been developed, much as the turkey was developed from the wild birds found by the American settlers. At what rate are you losing them, Chapman? No exaggeration now.'

Chapman said, 'Oh, about six or eight a week, and that is no my eye and Betty Martin!'

I inquired, 'They cannot fly out through the open top of the pen?'

Chapman laughed, 'Not a chance, your jungle fowl is no

flyer. At best he can rise four or five feet and break his fall with his wings. There are no perches high enough to aid an escape.'

Holmes asked, 'There are no predatory creatures loose at night?' He grinned, 'Only my cats and the rats they prey upon. A jungle fowl is more than a match for a rat, yes and even a cat for that matter. What is more there would be bones and feathers about if any of them had been killed and eaten.'

Despite his seeming minimal interest I noticed that Holmes's eyes were busy darting about him. They focused first upon the fanlight over the entrance door with its secure mesh cover, then moved along the cornice to observe the many spaces betwixt wall and ceiling. These were the access places of the rats, their way in from adjoining buildings; but their relevance had already been discounted. Then Holmes said, 'My dear Chapman, I shall dwell upon your problem. However, the inner man calls for support. Can you recommend an establishment where we can eat in the near proximity.' I opened my mouth and closed it again. It was true that the snack which we had taken at Simpsons had been of the lightest, but I knew the good Mrs Hudson would have a game pie for us back at Baker Street.

Chapman knew nothing of our recent repast and asked, 'Would you gentlemen have a liking for a good hot curry?'

I picked up my cue from Holmes, saying, 'Why yes, my service in Afghanistan gave me a taste for such delights.'

Within minutes we were seated at a table in Ali's Curry Palace which by chance actually abutted Chapman's premises. I do not imagine that many of my readers have experience of such an establishment, for in the British Isles the only popular exotic eating appears to lean toward the Chinese cuisine. The small neat be-turbaned owner of the Curry Palace placed the tips of his fingers together and inclined his body at the waist. 'Welcome sahibs, I will myself attend to your needs.'

Holmes smiled and stated, 'Mr Ali, I observe you are from Bombay.'

The Indian started a little, 'Sahib, how can you, an English gentleman, tell if I am from Bombay rather than perhaps Calcutta?'

Holmes replied, 'The salutation which you have given us is typical of Bombay. If from Calcutta you would have touched palms rather than fingertips and your bow would have been less pronounced.'

When the smiling Indian produced a menu Holmes chose for us mild curried chicken, though when it was produced he did little more than play with it. However, as a hearty trencherman I could not resist making a stab at eating my meal; managing perhaps half of it.

As I ate Holmes studied me carefully. He said, 'You have your uses, Watson! Tell me now, what is your opinion of the chicken curry?'

I said, 'Well I am bound to say that I find it excellent; there is not a scrap of fat upon the chicken, just good lean meat.'

He nodded his agreement, 'My own feeling from a smaller sampling than your own.'

At this point a diversion occurred as a small weasel-like animal suddenly scuttled across the floor of the café.

Full of apology Mr Ali captured it, chiding his waiter. 'You should have been sure that his cage was shut!' He spoke in Urdu, but I caught the gist of what he said. Then he spoke in English, 'My apologies sahibs, my pet is not usually allowed in this part of the building but keeps my kitchen clear of vermin.' Then he retreated toward his kitchen with the intriguing little creature writhing in his arms.

I turned to Holmes and said, 'Kipling's Riki Tiki Tavi, eh?'

He nodded, 'The grey mongoose, very popular as a pet in India, and more than a match for a cobra.'

Then, rather to my surprise Holmes expressed extreme delight with the curry in praising it to Mr Ali. 'An excellent fowl, my dear sir, and I wonder if I dare ask you how it is prepared?' Ali beckoned us to follow him into his kitchen where he proceeded to show us the manner of slicing and cooking the birds. But I noticed that Holmes's eyes were everywhere, particularly making darts toward a refuse bin which stood upon the floor. I noticed that there were chicken feathers, also heads and feet therein. The latter were interesting for the extra large spurs which they carried. Fine quality birds were obviously used.

On our way from the kitchen we passed the mongoose now safely in his hutch, where he crouched, surrounded by the remains of his meal of chicken wings with glossy red feathers not even plucked from them.

Outside in the street Holmes said to me quietly, 'I think we have solved the mystery of the disappearing jungle fowl, don't you, Watson?' I agreed, for whilst I do not suggest that I would have quite so easily solved the mystery on my own I had to admit that it was one of the easiest puzzles presented to the great detective. I said as much and Holmes said, 'Quite so, Watson, and it would have occurred to you to look for a nearby eating house when trying to establish a reason for the fowl diminishing in number?' Holmes can be very sardonic.

Soon we were back at Chapman's, where we gave the owner our findings. To my surprise Chapman burst out laughing. 'So he's been sending his mongoose through the rat runs to nab my fowl to turn into curry? Why the little blighter! You know, Mr Holmes, it is funny and most ingenious. What put you onto the answer?'

Holmes said, 'The presence of the rat runs, the proximity of the curry house and the sheer logic of it all. Mind you, had we not seen the mongoose it would have taken longer to solve. Then once I had seen the chicken feet with the red plumage and distinctive large spurs, bred out of domestic poultry, it was all elementary, especially with the very fine quality of the fowl used in the curry.'

I asked, 'What action shall you take, Chapman?'

The animal dealer laughed again at my words, 'Action? Why bless your heart, Doctor Watson, I will take none in law but will quickly put a mesh top on the fowl pen. That will put a stop to Riki Tiki's attention to my stock. If it does not, I will catch the little blighter, put him in a cage and sell him to a zoo!'

As we passed Ali's Curry Palace again on our way back to the Strand its owner was standing outside. He smiled and salaamed again and said, 'Farewell gentlemen, you are both going to be so lucky, I feel these things.'

Holmes smiled and replied, 'You should know Mr Ali, for you are, as it happens, a very lucky man yourself!'

The Incident of the Baker's Watch

During many years of acting as Boswell to my friend
Sherlock Holmes I have chronicled so many cases of his,
which have varied so much in their complexity and in their
presentation of difficulty or ease of solution. On the one
hand there were extremely baffling enigmas like that of the
ghostly hound on Dartmoor, which took up so much of the
detective's time and held a considerable element of danger,
for client and investigator alike. But there were problems
which whilst they involved the requirement of Holmes's
powers of deduction were very quickly solved. Such a case
was that of the Baker's watch. The reader may consider this
as a mere trifle when compared to some of our other
adventures yet I feel that it had points of interest making it
worthy of recording for posterity.

The puzzle, a seemingly minor one at first thought, was
brought to Holmes by one George Barret who arrived
without appointment or warning on one winter's night just
as we had finished our dinner and were seated by the fire
with cigars and liqueurs. Barret, despite this lack of warning, seemed rather confident in his manner, with something of the air of a long-lost friend. Holmes rose to greet
him, saying, 'Mr Barret, I do not usually conduct interviews
with those who are in need of my services save by prior

arrangement. The penny post is still operating and so is the wire system.'

'Mr Holmes, I know it has been a few years but do you really mean to say that you do not recognise or remember me?' Our visitor removed his cap and grinned from ear to ear, then suddenly there was something in his face that started to ring some bells in my brain. I glanced round at Holmes and could see from his expression that he had recognised our visitor.

He said, 'Upon my word, it is little George!' Of course, now I recognised the face with the broad grin, though I had to mentally transpose short porcupine hair onto his pomaded pate.

I gasped, 'Little George, a leading light of the Irregulars? Forgive me, George, but it has been more than a few years!' We both shook George Barret warmly by his strong right hand and for perhaps ten minutes we reminisced regarding the exploits of those street Arabs, himself among them, who perhaps a decade ago had been so instrumental in helping Holmes to bring many a criminal to justice. Then of course we started to ask him questions concerning the ten years when he had been lost to us. He decided to tell us the whole story.

'I was a wrong 'un when I first met you two gents, if you remember, but the trust you placed in me, and those little rewards that you gave me in return for doing a bit of shadowing and the like saved me from the house of correction. After a couple of years it must have seemed to you that I just disappeared. Maybe you thought that I had gone back to thieving and got myself arrested for it, or so busy that you did not even think about it? But far from a life of crime I went for a soldier, a drummer boy at first, then an artillery man and eventually a sergeant. I got that promotion through the training that you gave me, Mr Holmes, rather than from anything that the army showed me. I seemed to stand out from the other private soldiers from my ability to make deductions.

'Your methods made it seem to them that I had second sight in my ability to out-think the enemy. I'll tell you, Mr Holmes, had you decided on an army career you would have made colonel in a month and general within a couple of years. Though come to think of it, the regular daily routine might have driven you mad! However, I'm gettin' sideswiped, ain't I?

'To cut a long story short along came the Boer War and I copped a leg wound from some Voortrekker's rifle, and got sent home. I was discharged from the army on medical grounds, with a bit of a gratuity. Instead of spending it on ale and betting like most of them do, I got myself a barrow and sold bread and cakes in the street.'

Holmes sat quietly listening to Barret's narration but could not resist an interruption at this point. 'My dear Barret, I deduce that you did not stop at selling bread and cakes but eventually took to making them yourself?'

George Barret turned to me with a ghost of the Irregulars' impish grin and said, 'He's still at it, Doctor. He may have lost a little hair but none of his brains!'

Holmes smoothed back his thinning widow's peak with the fingers of his right hand, saying, 'Hardly a gigantic deduction, my dear Barret, to recognise the pallor typical of the baker. Notice, Watson, despite his healthy frame he has a complexion brought about by the fact that no amount of soap and water will eliminate the flour entirely from the pores. But tell me, George, is there a Mrs Barret to share your work and your good fortune?'

By way of answer George recommenced his narration. 'Remember little Flossie, with the flowered bonnet and dirty face who was always hanging around with the Irregulars? Well, she grew up to be a regular beauty. She wrote to me regular, all the time I was in the army like, and we became engaged just before the war broke out with the Boers. Then when I came out, with my gratuity, we were able to be wed and — yes — she has made a wonderful baker's mate. Being pale suits a woman better than it does a bloke, Mr Holmes!'

I said at this point, 'I really do congratulate you, my dear Barret, upon your marriage and also upon your enterprise. But forgive me, was it just an overwhelming desire to see us again that brought you to 221b tonight?'

Holmes looked at me rather reproachfully, 'Oh come, Watson, it is our good fortune that George decided to visit us. The reason for his visit could have something to do with the fact that he has recently inherited a watch and possibly another object which he has brought with him. The watch is of little value and in point of fact is not even running.'

Barret's face was a study at these words. He said, 'Well bless me sir, I inherited the watch that I am wearing from an uncle recently deceased. He also left me his stamp collection. How you knew of the low value of the timepiece or that it does not work I can't imagine.'

Holmes chuckled. 'I noticed the chain upon your waistcoat as soon as you came in. Its quality is such that one would not normally use it to ensure the safety of an expensive timepiece.'

I could not but interrupt, 'How did you know that the watch was not running?'

He grinned again. 'George several times has glanced at the clock, which required some contortions of the neck and shoulders from where he is seated. Normally one would under such circumstances consult one's own watch. Such a practical man would normally leave the watch at home were he not wearing it as a mark of tribute. The package under his arm might also be connected with the inheritance. It is in fact a stamp album.'

Barret was delighted, 'Right all along the line sir. The watch is a five-bob Ensign and it doesn't work — in fact I cannot even get the back open to get it running. But as you suggest I thought I would wear it for a day or two out of respect. The spring is not broken as I know from the winder, only a watch maker will, I imagine, be able to open it without harming the watch, so I will take it to old Johnson in a day or so.'

Holmes said, 'Hardly worth the mending, but a keepsake eh?'

Barret displayed the cheap Ensign watch on the palm of his hand, 'Yes, it is practically without value save to remember my uncle by, which is why I was very surprised indeed when someone tried to steal it.'

Holmes started, 'What! When was this?'

George said, 'This very morning, I was just taking a stroll near my home when a pickpocket tried to nab it.'

Holmes asked, 'An urchin of the Artful Dodger variety?'

He answered, 'Why no, it was a grown man who looked like he could have been a professional.'

'Upon my word' ... Holmes mused ... 'what expert would risk being caught in the attempt to steal a watch on a chain like that?' Holmes charged his pipe with the shag from the Turkish slipper but grunted in annoyance as he noticed that it was all but empty. 'Watson would you not be a good fellow and fetch me some shag from the tobacconist? I believe he will still be open if you hurry.' I made to prepare to go, but Barret insisted on going instead.

George thrust the package into Holmes's hands as he rose to prepare for his errand. 'Take a look at these stamps, Mr Holmes, I think you'll reckon them about as valuable as the watch.' He left briskly to get the tobacco.

Holmes carefully removed the album from its brown paper and idly turned the pages to look at the serried rows of colourful stamps, arranged upon headed sheets of paper. 'As Barret stated, these are of about the same value as the watch!' Then he suddenly came upon a page which had a space amid an otherwise filled row. There was a clear hinge left adhering to the paper where a stamp had been removed. He took his lens to it, grunted and closed the album. As he made to wrap it again, he glanced at the inside of the brown paper. He noticed something that interested him. He said, 'Watson, be good enough to pass to me one of the soft pencils which you will find upon the mantelpiece.'

As I handed him the pencil and wondered why he needed it, my thoughts were interrupted by the return of George Barret. He entered the room briskly, all but threw the screw of paper containing the shag into my hands and said, 'You will find it hard to believe what I am about to tell you, gentlemen! After my visit to the tobacconist I was on my way back here when someone tried to purloin my watch. That makes twice within a couple of days or so that someone has chanced his arm for the sake of a dollar Ensign!'

'What?' Holmes put down the brown paper and pencil and wheeled to face Barret. 'Was it the same person who tried it before?'

He said, 'Why no, this fellow was a shifty looking little man with a mole upon his nose.'

I caught Holmes's eye and murmured 'Swifty Manners?'

He nodded, 'Place the watch carefully upon the table, George, whilst I investigate the inside of this wrapper. There is the impression from something written with a sharp pencil upon a paper, rested on the wrapper.'

The detective deftly rubbed the soft pencil over the impression with just the right amount of pressure required to reveal a message. 'George, you will find the Mauritius in time. . .' Barret and I could not immediately make any sense of the message, but there was a look of triumph in Holmes's hawk-like eyes.

'Watson, somewhere upon that shelf next to the row of files there is a book upon the subject of foreign stamps. Be good enough to pass it to me.' I soon found the book he wanted; it was a sort of manual upon the subject of philately with illustrations of rare examples doubtless to bring joy to those with an interest in collecting postage stamps. He quickly turned the pages and revealed a picture of a stamp with a bird depicted upon it and marked Mauritius. He read the printed message beneath it and then placed the book aside. 'Your uncle left you a valuable stamp, George, but did not trust it to the album. He wrote a message for you to give a clue as to its whereabouts. I have produced an impression of that message, but you do not have the original?'

George shook his head. 'When I went to his home to claim the items his housekeeper picked up a scrap of paper which fell from the album when I unwrapped it. She said it was just a piece of plain paper and she screwed it up and dropped it in the waste basket. Do you think maybe . . . ?'

Holmes did not wait for his next words, 'Yes, I do!'

George said, 'Mrs Sparks has always struck me as being a highly respectable lady.'

Holmes snapped, 'Maybe she is, but she evidently has some shifty friends.'

Holmes unwrapped the fresh tobacco and dispensed it into the Turkish slipper prior to filling his pipe from it. We had to sit upon the edges of our chairs and wait whilst he lit it with a hot coal from the fire held in the tongs. Having lit the pipe to his satisfaction he sat and puffed thoughtfully for a while. Neither of us dared disturb his reverie. Then, at last, he said, 'Your uncle was fond of puzzles, George?'

Barret said, 'Why yes, at Christmas he would entertain us for hours with riddles and puzzles.'

Holmes said, 'Well, the Mauritius is a rare stamp, worth thousands of pounds. "You will find it in time," which I begin to suspect suggests in a watch. He placed the stamp inside the cheap watch which he also left to you. This caused the watch to stop and also caused at least two of the housekeeper's friends to want to purloin it. Please, Barret, place the watch on the table, for I don't think we need to wait for you to take it to the watch maker.'

Sherlock Holmes took the watch in his hands and then to my amazement banged it upon the table with such force that the hinged back flew open despite the impediment that had jammed it. A small colourful paper square fluttered from it and, in the same instant, the cheap mechanism started to tick.

In turn we consulted the stamp manual which gave the information that the Mauritius stamp before us was very rare and valuable indeed. The detective handled the stamp carefully, placing it into a small transparent envelope, bidding Barret to lodge it carefully in his wallet. 'Take it to Gibbons in the Strand, Barret. He will treat you fairly as to price.'

I remonstrated, 'I had better escort George home and tomorrow to Gibbons, without forgetting to carry my service revolver!'

But Holmes laughed at my concern. 'My dear Watson, Barret's stamp will be secure in his wallet. The watch and chain will prove a perfect decoy!'

As it transpired George Barret got safely to Gibbons with the stamp for which he got a fair price involving several thousand pounds. That, dear reader, is how one of the Irregulars not only grew from a shifty urchin into a respectable citizen but ultimately came to own one of the finest bakery businesses in the centre of London.

All This and the Giant Rat of Sumatra!

'The fun of the fair' has never appealed to my tastes and one could be forgiven for thinking that the same would be true of my friend and colleague Mr Sherlock Holmes, the eminent consulting detective of 221b Baker Street. But I suppose there was something in the bizarre nature of such a collection of stalls and side shows that interested him. I had scarce thought about this until upon a particular Easter bank holiday he suggested a walk upon Hampstead Heath. I had quite forgotten the long-established funfair held there upon such days, but in retrospect I do believe that it was in Holmes's mind to visit this exhibition of tented wonders before we started out. 'Bless my soul, a fair!' He was not very convincing in his expression of surprise.

We wandered among the attractions for a while and Holmes treated me to his views upon how the public were being hoodwinked into paying to try and dislodge a coconut and how their pennies, rolled down a chute, could not for good scientific reasons fall to cover the numbers upon a printed cloth. He knew the devices used by the thimble riggers, cheap jacks and three-card-trick shysters to an extent that began to depress me. I longed to find some enterprise which offered exactly what it advertised, with no sort of chicanery. At last we found such a one.

At the far end of the fairground area we came upon one of those relics of a bygone age of bestiality, a freak show. Outside a marquee of fairly modest size stood a pale-faced man of considerable build wearing a particularly loud checked suit of clothes, rather like those worn by street turf accountants that their trade might be obvious to those with wagers to make. He wore a grey derby hat, and brandished a cane in one hand, holding a megaphone in the other. With the cane he gesticulated toward a cloth banner which bore the words:

TEMPLE OF WONDERS!
SEE THE MOST HORRIFIC COLLECTION OF FREAKS
EVER ASSEMBLED

The unsavoury-looking man raised his megaphone and through it he began to shout, punctuating his remarks with spasmodic swipes at the banner with his cane. 'Ladies and gentlemen, within this temple of wonders you will be able to see the original Siamese Twins, joined at the waist from birth. Also the fattest woman ever exhibited, Jolly Daisy tips the scales at forty-seven stone. If you don't believe me just take a look at these!' He held up an item of female attire not usually mentioned by name in a family publication. 'She fills them to bursting point.' He cast aside the tent-like garment and swiped again with his cane. 'See the smallest man in the world, General Attila, only twenty-eight inches tall at twenty-three years old. See Hans the Giganticus, the tallest man in Europe, if not the world.

Hans measures almost nine feet! All alive, ladies and gentlemen, not models but these real living wonders before your very eyes. All this and the Giant Rat of Sumatra. Forty inches from nose to tail tip, the largest rat ever captured, let alone exhibited!'

This singularly unpleasant-seeming individual went on to announce that all these wonders could be seen for three pence only, or three halfpence for children and servants.

I turned to Holmes and asked, 'A deception I suppose, not genuine freaks of nature?'

But rather to my surprise he shook his head, 'I doubt it, Watson, there are enough poor deformed examples of humanity to keep the showmen in business without need to resort to deception. I think you will find that there has been some very slight exaggeration regarding measurements, but largely these attractions will be genuine.'

I was all for passing on to some more tasteful attraction, but Holmes insisted that I should see for myself that his words were true. Yes and true they were for as a medical man I could see that the enormously stout woman was at least thirty-five stone, and the twenty-eight-inch man no more than two and a half feet high. The Siamese Twins were individuals above the waist, where they were joined and shared a single pair of legs. The giant so called was typical of his kind, with overdeveloped jaw and huge hands. He certainly was in excess of eight feet in height, but betrayed the frailty of those who suffer from this glandular irregularity; a size not even matched by puny strength.

There were in addition a few glass aquaria containing reptiles, for instance a large snake and of course the famous Giant Rat of Sumatra which Holmes assured me was nutria of perfectly normal size for its species. 'Sometimes called coypu, it actually originates from South America rather than Sumatra. But it is enough like the domestic rat to have long been popular with showmen as an exhibit. I saw one once which it was claimed had been captured in the sewers of Paris. A throwback to the days of the Franco-Prussian war when the Parisians had to eat rats!'

The daylight had deserted the scene and a sudden driving rain made difficulty for the showmen with their naphtha flares. Soon most of the attractions were closed and we repaired to the inn on the heath. Due to the increasingly inclement weather we stayed there longer than we had intended, until in fact at about ten of the clock people began to enter the inn with stories of some sort of tragic event upon the fairground. I asked one of them, 'Sir, what is the incident upon the heath?'

He replied, 'The cove in charge of the freak show has been strangled. They think, the rozzers that is, that one of his exhibits did it, for he was known to be cruel to all of them!'

Holmes and I exchanged glances and he answered my unspoken question. 'Why yes, Watson, I think we should return to the fairground at once.'

The freak show tent was surrounded by police constables and a sergeant stopped us at the entrance flap. Holmes showed him his visiting card and I wondered if this would cause him to allow us to enter. As it happened it did and he said, 'Sherlock Holmes, eh? I've followed your adventures in *The Strand* for years, I feel sure that the inspector will be glad of your help.'

Inside the tent a stable lantern hung and cast an eerie

illumination. We could see that the freaks each had a camp bed, as if all preparation for a normal end to the day had been made. These beds had evidently been especially made, being each of suitable size for the exhibit concerned. But these unfortunates either sat or stood beside their cots in a rather bewildered picture. At the far end of the tent there was a small caravan, with its small entrance door open, likewise its only tiny window. With one foot on the caravan steps there lounged Inspector Cresswell of Scotland Yard. He recognised us at once and said, 'Why, Mr Holmes, Doctor Watson, what a surprise. I feel sure that you have had a wasted journey from Baker Street, for this is what we call an open-and-shut case. These strange people had bedded down for the night, likewise the showman in his caravan. We have plenty of witnesses from outside to make it clear that no one entered the tent. One of these freaks entered the caravan and strangled the showman. I have spoken with them all and each of them had reason to hate him. The only question is which one of them was it, and did they collude upon the crime?'

Holmes asked, 'One of them must have raised the alarm.'

He replied, 'Yes, well it would be the more suspicious if they did not, what?'

Holmes asked if we might see the body and the inspector agreed that we might. 'But you won't touch anything eh?'

We nodded our assent and mounted the steps, wriggling our way through the extremely small entrance door. The showman lay, wearing his pyjamas, on a cot which folded against one side of the vehicle. His colour was such and his eyes enough distended for me to diagnose strangulation without need of further examination. Holmes nodded when I gave him this opinion. He said to the inspector, 'And you consider that one of his exhibits has done this to him?'

He replied, 'Yes, would you like to question them?'

Holmes shook his head, 'There is no need, for none of them could have done it.'

The inspector started, 'How can you tell me that without more investigation?'

Holmes said, 'Let us consider them in turn. The little man who raised the alarm would not have had the strength in his tiny hands to strangle even a chicken!'

The inspector grunted. 'Well how about the Siamese Twins?'

Holmes chuckled grimly, 'How on earth could these unfortunates, joined at the waist, have entered through an aperture which I, wiry as I am, had to negotiate with care. It goes without saying that the huge woman could not be suspected, even vaguely. This leaves only the giant.' He shrugged as if to indicate the obvious.

Suddenly Cresswell brightened, 'I have it, the giant could not have entered through the door but he has very long arms and he could reach the showman through that little window!'

Holmes looked at the small aperture and said, 'He might have extended one arm with its one hand through that far but this has been done by a much stronger agency than the single hand of debilitated man. I think Watson, as a medical man, will agree that he would not have managed it.'

I nodded my agreement, and the inspector glared at us both. 'I wouldn't be too sure, until the police surgeon has confirmed all this. But just as a matter of interest, if none of the freaks have strangled him, who then? Some invisible man or unearthly spirit?'

Sherlock Holmes paced restlessly inside the tent and looked at everything he saw. He stopped at the row of aquaria. Cresswell asked, sardonically, 'Don't tell me that you think he was strangled by the Giant Rat of Sumatra?'

Holmes laughed, without malice. 'No, but if you look into the adjoining tank which housed a python of considerable size, I think all might be made clear.'

The inspector gasped; he could see a vague possibility in these words. 'The snake is missing! Could it have done this?'

Holmes nodded, 'It is a constricting snake; it could have wound itself around his neck and killed him most easily in a manner that would look more like an obvious strangulation by a human agency. Moreover, it could have entered through the tiny window when the door was closed.'

Holmes took the top off the tank and examined the interior. 'The creature made its exit through a carelessly opened ventilation panel.' He took his lens from his pocket and examined the floor of the case. Taking out a small specimen envelope he carefully deposited in it some fragments of skin. 'The creature was, or is, sloughing its skin. I think your surgeon might find some traces of such scales near the neck of the victim.'

When, later, the police surgeon had examined the body and emerged from the caravan he said, 'He was certainly strangled and it was recently. The neck bruising is consistent with this and there are some minute pieces of skin upon the pillow which look as if they might be from the hands of someone suffering from some rare tropical skin disease.'

He displayed some scraps of skin-like substance in a transparent envelope.

Inspector Cresswell asked, 'Could it be snakeskin?'

The surgeon considered, 'It could!'

When Holmes had surrendered his own snakeskin samples the surgeon agreed that they were identical.

The police, ourselves and even the freaks conducted a search for the python and it was eventually found curled up in the centre of some bales of straw. The inspector was for having it shot, but before the sentence could be carried out the fat lady had lifted the snake, with amazing strength and agility, and returned it to its tank. From the way it reacted it was obvious that the creature knew her well.

Back at Baker Street as we enjoyed a late night drink I asked Holmes, 'Do you suppose that the fat woman could have trained the python to kill the showman and released it with this in mind?'

Holmes very carefully filled a clay with the Scottish mixture before he replied, 'Watson, I do not discount the possibility.' He applied a lit vesta to the tobacco and filled his surroundings with acrid smoke before delivering his last words on the subject. 'Enough to say that I feel sure that this thought will not occur to the police, and I have interfered in their affairs too much already to consider suggesting it!'

The Lobster Quadrille

'By Jove! If it isn't old Watson! What ho, old boy, haven't seen you in donkey's years!'

I was strolling in Baker Street when the once familiar stentorian voice assaulted my ear drums. I had not seen Colonel Archibald Fanshawe since serving under him in Afghanistan, where he had been a good and fair-minded commanding officer despite certain eccentricities. For example, he was forever trying to suggest to his colleagues that he was a good deal younger than we knew him to be. Now he was a little changed by the passing of fifteen years, for though still upright and hearty his face was somewhat lined. Though to counteract this, his once grizzled hair and whiskers were now a striking auburn colour.

He continued, 'Still got the gammy leg I see, and you've got the odd grey hair.' I refrained from mentioning his own obvious application of henna. 'Got married since I came out of the service, Watters, and a darned good-looking filly she is too. You must meet her. Where are you digging?'

I told him that I was sharing rooms with my friend Sherlock Holmes at 221b Baker Street.

He asked, 'You mean the detective johnny? By Jove! I'd love to meet him, and I know Mavis would too — that is the memsahib, you know. Why don't you both come to dinner with us on Thursday night, we'll have a lobster quadrille!'

I enquired, 'What is a lobster quadrille?'

He said, 'Forgotten your Lewis Carroll, what? Well, we'll have lobster, and there would be just the four of us, so hence lobster quadrille!' He gave me his card and I promised to try and get Holmes to join us for a lobster dinner.

I had often mentioned Archie Fanshawe to Sherlock Holmes when speaking of my adventures in Afghanistan but knowing how very unsociable he could be I was surprised that he agreed to join us at dinner on the Thursday night involved. He said, 'Come! I am fond of lobster, Watson, but I feel sure that Colonel Fanshawe will be well aware of the dangers involved in eating them.'

On the appointed night and time we arrived at Fanshawe's flat in George Street, which was so close to 221b as to make the hansom we employed hardly necessary. Holmes, to my surprise, dressed carefully in his tails and dress cravat. But then the world's first consulting detective was always full of surprises. Though not of a sociable nature, his manners were always impeccable, especially where the fair sex was involved. Women had no part to play in his life but he always treated them with a charming old-world courtesy. He bowed as we shook hands with Mavis, the wife of Colonel Archibald Fanshawe.

I confess that with the sure knowledge that Archie was, despite his auburn locks, at least sixty-five years old, I was expecting to be introduced to a lady of fairly mature years. Instead Mavis Fanshawe was perhaps eight-and-twenty, with wonderful dark tresses and a face and figure to be envied by any picture-postcard beauty. Charming too, she put us both at our ease and smiled engagingly as she dispensed our aperitif. 'Archie and I like to live quietly so we chose this compact apartment and we retain just the one servant, James. We manage very well with a little help from a couple of charwomen who come in during the mornings.' She was a good hostess and, considering her tiny ménage, a resourceful one.

After James had served a fruit compote he cleared the empty dishes to allow room to display the four lobsters, or Lobster Quadrille as Archie Fanshawe had called the dish. He brought them to the table in a basket. All four of them were lively enough to show that they had not been many hours out of the ocean. 'Pick whichever you would like Holmes, and Watson. I always like to choose a lobster, don't you?' I said that so long as the lobster was alive and kicking up to the time of its cooking I would be happy. Holmes said the same.

Mavis played along with Archie and selected one with some barnacles still on its shell, and Archie chose one which appeared to have a couple of malformed legs. 'Y'know some of the fishermen catch lobsters and throw them back after chopping off the odd leg. The little blighters grow fresh legs, so it's all rather economical really, what?'

James took the basket of lobsters away to the kitchen, from where we heard the bubbling of the water and the four distinct screams as the lobsters were dropped into the cruel seething water.

Fanshawe leaned across and said, 'Cracking good chap, James! You know he is the sole support of his elderly parents. Don't know how he manages on what I pay him, eh what?' We just nodded, Holmes with seeming uninterest and I with just a hint of a polite smile. Then James entered with a soufflé which he had evidently prepared for us to sample whilst the lobsters were cooking. As he disappeared back into the kitchen Holmes muttered to me under his breath, 'James wears a splendid diamond ring and cuff links worth hundreds!'

I mumbled, 'None of our business, what?'

Mavis Fanshawe was the perfect hostess, keeping the wine circulating and the conversation going. She even managed to get some animation from Sherlock Holmes when she raised the subject of the perfect crime.

Holmes said, 'The only crime which can be called perfect, at least as far as murder is concerned, is that which imitates natural causes and does not excite investigation. I have been involved in a number of cases involving arsenic poisoning which is notoriously difficult to prove. There are various quite everyday sources of arsenic, including spinach. Where a large quantity of spinach has been habitually consumed it would take only a very small dose of arsenic to cause death by poisoning.'

Mavis Fanshawe seemed fascinated by Holmes's words, saying, 'So if this woman wanted to murder her husband she would feed him spinach every day and then administer a small quantity of weed killer in his soup?'

Holmes nodded, then said, 'However, in my experience the wife has more often been the victim.' I fancied I saw him catch her eye for just a second.

The conversation was interrupted by the presentation by James of the lobsters. They were in their shells — as is usual in the best of establishments — and this made it possible for me to notice that Fanshawe was served with the lobster of his choice; the one with the limbs mis-shapened by regrowth. Mavis was served with the one with barnacle scars upon its shell. The sauce was in a large bowl from which we each helped ourselves by means of a ladle.

As I squeezed some lemon on to some of the lobster meat I felt bound to congratulate Mavis Fanshawe upon the dish. 'Really excellent, Mrs Fanshawe. These lobsters beat those that I have had straight from the sea at St Ives.' She inclined her head and smiled, emphasising her brilliant beauty.

It took us a very long time to feast upon our lobsters which we all did with avid relish, save for Colonel Fanshawe. He attacked his lobster with activity at first, but when he had consumed quite a lot of it he slowed down and I fancied he looked a little unwell. Then he took the handkerchief from his display pocket and said huskily, 'Feelin' a little bit feverish, must be in for another dose of malaria, Mavis.' He dabbed at his brow, drank some wine, and then suddenly he slumped forward on to the table.

I raised him up and made a lightning examination. His breath was coming in short gasps and his eyes were protruding alarmingly. He clutched at his middle region and gasped, 'I'm dying, old man . . . can't be the lobster . . .' then he lost consciousness and I tried to revive him.

I said to Holmes, 'Ambulance, quickly, or he'll be a goner!'

But Holmes had anticipated this need and was already struggling into his evening cape. He said, 'Do what you can for him, Watson, I'll get help.'

I had not, obviously, brought my medical bag, but I did

what I could for him, trying without much success to induce regurgitation. Mavis was icy calm and did what she could to help me. She also kept saying, 'Archie, it is going to be fine, just hold on!' Then, after what seemed like an age, the ambulance men arrived and took Fanshawe away on a stretcher. Mavis made to follow them but was held from doing so by the return of Sherlock Holmes. He said, 'Mrs Fanshawe, he is in good hands, and I would appreciate that you stay and listen to what I have to say.' He deposited a package in grease-proof paper upon a chair in the corner of the room as Mavis obeyed his suggestion and sat at the table, her expression one of curiosity.

Holmes sat opposite to her at the table which still bore the remains of the lobster quadrille, as poor old Archie Fanshawe had termed it. Holmes spoke quietly but urgently. 'Your husband is, I believe, dying from shell-fish poisoning.' He turned to me, 'Would you make that diagnosis, Watson?'

I agreed. 'On the limited examination that was possible.'

He continued, 'I must tell you, Mrs Fanshawe, that I have sent for the police.'

She started, 'That must mean that you suspect foul play!'

I also remonstrated, 'Come, Holmes, surely you are jumping to conclusions.'

He answered my question with one of his own, 'Have you ever known me to jump to conclusions, Watson?' I had, on reflection, to murmur to the effect that I had not. Holmes continued, 'All four lobsters were alive when we were allowed to choose one. Poisoning could not really have resulted from eating the flesh of a lobster which was as fresh, yet Fanshawe exhibited all the symptoms of shell-fish poisoning. I can only conclude that the lobster he chose was contaminated in some way.'

At this point two police constables arrived and were admitted by James. To my surprise they were accompanied by an old colleague of ours, Inspector Gregson. He explained that he had happened to be at the local police station when Holmes's request for police presence was stated. 'As soon as I heard that you were involved, Mr Holmes, I thought I'd better look in. I understand that you sent for the police as well as an ambulance?'

Holmes nodded, 'I'm very pleased to see you, my dear Gregson. You will reduce my responsibility in this matter.'

Holmes informed Gregson concerning the whole unfortunate incident including the incidents of the selection of live lobsters and their evident cooking whilst still alive. He blanched at the thought, saying, 'Thank the Lord I am of that station in life where a piece of fresh cod and some chipped potatoes are a delicacy. Where did you purchase the lobsters, Mrs Fanshawe?'

She answered, 'From Billings on the corner; an excellent fish shop from which we have often had live lobsters before.'

Gregson turned to Holmes. 'Is it possible that a substitution of the freshly cooked lobster was made?'

Holmes was about to reply when Mavis Fanshawe butted in, 'Inspector, my guests will confirm that Archie chose the lobster with which he was served and that it has a very distinctive appearance which he remarked upon himself.'

I said, 'He chose the one with the deformed legs because I remember that he told us that its legs had been removed, the lobster returned to the sea from which it had been caught again after growing new ones. Mrs Fanshawe also chose a lobster that could be easily recognised from its shell.'

Gregson enquired, 'Did you cook the lobsters, Mrs Fanshawe?'

She replied, 'No, our servant, James, placed them into the boiling water whilst I kept my guests entertained. Mr Holmes will remember the four screams that were heard as the creatures were dropped into the utensil in which they were boiled. They were brought straight out here as soon as they were ready, still in their shells.'

Gregson questioned the sauce, which Mavis claimed to have made herself, and she sampled a spoonful to show her confidence in it. Then he turned to Holmes and said, 'You have still not answered my question concerning how any substitution might have been made.'

My friend closed his eyes as he answered, as if attempting a recitation and being fearful of forgetting a line. He said, 'James, I do not know your other name.'

The servant answered, 'Grant, my name is James Grant.'

Holmes carried on, 'Well, James Grant, you cooked the lobsters but did not Mrs Fanshawe have some hand in their preparation?'

He said, 'Why no, I did it all on my own, sir.'

Holmes said, 'So you loosened the flesh in the shells before serving the lobsters?'

He said, 'Yes, that is usual. We have a special knife for doing it.'

Gregson was interested now. 'Were the lobsters taken out of their shells at any stage?'

James said, 'No, that is not necessary, they were just loosened.'

Holmes indicated the lobster which the colonel had partaken. 'Yet the flesh of this one is so loose that it can be lifted out.' He demonstrated with the aid of a fork.

James said, 'I must have been a little bit overactive with the knife.'

Holmes examined the other lobsters and showed that what flesh was left in them was still attached to the shell base. He said, 'You showed that activity only in the case of the colonel's lobster?'

James spluttered, 'What are you trying to suggest? I was just doing my job.'

Holmes sat back in his chair, 'You made a substitution did you not, discarding the fresh lobster from its shell and replacing it with flesh that was several days old?'

James started, 'Why would I do that and even if I did where is the fresh lobster? Come, you can search the kitchen.'

Holmes grunted, 'I do not need to but I know that there is a door from the kitchen which gives access to the dustbin. I saw that when I went for the ambulance. I found a package containing the flesh of a fresh lobster just under the lid. This caused me to also send for the police. On a chair you will find the fresh lobster flesh, inspector. If you take the remains of the colonel's lobster to your scientific people you will be able to get some idea of its age.'

Gregson said, 'I have heard enough, Mr Holmes, to take some action in this matter.' He turned to the manservant. 'James Grant, I arrest you on suspicion of attempted murder of one Colonel Fanshawe.'

He was interrupted by Mavis. 'Inspector, anything James did was through following my instructions but of course there was no intent to murder!'

Gregson replied by saying, 'Mrs Fanshawe, I arrest you on suspicion of conspiracy with one James Grant to murder Colonel Fanshawe!'

'How is your friend, the colonel?' It was two days later and I had been to the hospital to see poor old Archie.

I answered Holmes's question, 'Poorly, but very much alive. He will be on his feet within a few days.'

He nodded, 'Glad to hear it. I imagine the man, Grant, will get a prison sentence but possibly the woman will get away with it.'

Holmes's words turned out to be accurate. The trial revealed that Grant and Mavis had in fact conspired to kill Colonel Fanshawe for the money which she knew that would be left to her in his will. She did not quite get away with it, but due to Archie's intervention she got the lightest of sentences and I felt that I knew that he would be waiting to forgive her and take up their life together when she emerged from prison.

The last words in the matter must be those of Sherlock Holmes: 'Many a young woman marries an elderly man for his money but fortunately most of them are patient enough to wait for his natural death. No doubt Grant made her agree to hasten the process. He was foolish in wearing the expensive presents that she had given him but the colonel was mesmerised by her to the extent that he would scarcely have noticed them.'

Sherlock Holmes and the Gypsy Switch

It was a pleasant summer evening and Sherlock Holmes, rather than taking advantage of the glorious twilight, insisted on staying in and playing his violin. I always had a problem with this particular talent of my friend's. I have never been musical enough to know just how good a musician Holmes was. Of course I am not completely tone deaf and even *I* could tell when he was playing an incorrect note — which he hardly ever did — but as for his standard of excellence as a violinist, I had no idea. At length he put down his instrument, peering out of the window, saying, 'I do believe we have a visitor, Watson.'

I was relieved, for enough violin music had been played for one evening as far as I was concerned.

Our caller turned out to be an elderly lady, her voice and dress suggesting that she was of the serving class. Her name was Mrs Joan Moran, and Holmes, always a perfect gentleman in his dealings with the fair sex whatever their station in life, bowed her into the most comfortable chair. When Mrs Hudson brought us a pot of tea and left it on the small brass-topped table that I had brought back from Afghanistan, Mrs Moran, as if from habit, started to pour and serve us. I was a little embarrassed but Holmes chuckled and his eyes twinkled as he said, 'Upon my word, Mrs Moran, it is a treat for a couple of old fogies like Watson and me to have a lady present when we are taking our tea but please, I beg you, do allow me to bring your cup to you. Then, when you have rested and refreshed yourself, you can tell me what it is that brings you to see me. By the way, my old friend and colleague Doctor Watson will not, as I forbid him to, publicise your business in the *Strand Magazine*, so you may speak freely!'

She smiled a little at his friendly jest and so the troubled expression on her face relaxed a little. She began her story, and Holmes leaned forward in his chair to assure her of his attention and interest. 'Well, Mr Holmes, I hardly know just where to start but I suppose the beginning is a good place. I am a widow and, as my husband left me a small annuity, I am able to live very carefully without want. But I have a friend, Mrs Cosgrove, who has recently lost her man and is not as well placed as I, having to take in washing to survive. She and I spend quite a lot of time together and I help her where I can. After all, if you can't help your friends it's a poor do, is it not?'

I cleared my throat impatiently, but Holmes turned and glared at me, 'Please, Watson. I am listening to Mrs Moran!'

But she took the hint and sped along with her narrative. 'Well, to cut a long story short, Mr Holmes, she and I went to see a demonstration by a Mr Ahmed Bey — an Arab he is — and he claims to bring down the spirits of lost relatives and friends. The meeting was in a church hall in Streatham, near where I live. He kept going into what he called a trance and seemed to be talking to various people around him, but you couldn't see none of them.

There was an Uncle George who he said wanted to speak to someone, and sure enough there was someone there who had an uncle named George who had passed on, as he put it.'

Holmes said, 'Why yes, I'm sure there was.'

Mrs Moran continued, 'He named a lot of spirits and although we never saw them there were lots of people sure that their dear ones were trying to get in touch. Then my friend heard from her Herbert, and this Ahmed Bey said for her to stay and talk to him after the meeting. Naturally we stayed, both of us. He took us into a back room and we sat down and he told us that he was going to give us a private consultation which would usually cost five guineas but he would do it for nothing.'

Holmes caught my eye as he said, 'How very generous.'

Then Mrs Moran told us how Ahmed went into another trance and when he came out of it she said he had held a long conversation with Herbert about her friend's future. 'He said that although he had not left her very well provided for he was about to rectify this. He said that if she were to place a gold sovereign in a handkerchief and bury it in the churchyard, just beside the oak tree, he would double its value.'

· I felt bound to ask, 'Did she do as he asked?'

She said, 'Yes, Doctor, and on the following morning she dug up the handkerchief and found two gold sovereigns in it! We went back to the Ahmed person again and he was delighted, and said that Herbert wanted her to repeat the whole thing, but with three sovereigns. Well do you know, eventually she dug up the handkerchief and found six sovereigns. It seemed that no matter how much was placed in the handkerchief and buried, Herbert would cause it to double in value. He suggested that she put fifty gold pieces in a handkerchief and that way she could make a nice little nest egg.

'Well, Mr Holmes I've explained how poor Herbert had left her with practically nothing. But it really did seem as if he were going to make up for it at last. I am not very well off but I managed to borrow from several friends until we had the fifty gold pieces like he said we needed. I went with her to the churchyard and we buried them in a handkerchief like before. Then came this morning when we went to the churchyard and dug it up. Do you know there was not only no doubling of her money but the money she had wrapped up was gone too. Nothing was there save a handkerchief. I thought perhaps a thief had taken it in the night but my friend said Herbert was punishing her for being greedy! Trouble is, I have to pay back everything that I have borrowed, and some of those who lent me the money will need it themselves.'

Holmes looked thoughtful as he asked, 'Have you taxed this Ahmed Bey with the situation?'

Mrs Moran said, 'Yes, but he refuses to accept any responsibility for the loss of the money. He says that once in a while it happens that the spirits decide to make mischief. Do you think I might be able to pawn or sell my necklace, Mr Holmes? There are one or two charms upon it that cost Herbert a pound or two.'

She unclipped her necklace by inserting her fingers under her hair at the back and held it up for us to see. It appeared to be gold plated but not of much value although some of the gold and silver plated charms were attractive enough, particularly those of a sphinx head and another of a silver crescent moon.

Holmes inspected it carefully before saying, 'Dear lady, I would keep the necklace, at least for the present, pending certain enquiries that I intend to make. I suggest that you return one week from this day and I will inform you regarding my progress.'

After she had left us Holmes explained to me something of the nature of the fraud which had evidently been perpetrated upon Mrs Moran. 'You see, Watson, money increases once, twice — three times even — all the time that the stakes are small but, as soon as the victim places a substantial sum in the handkerchief, this Ahmed Bey will remove it and then fob the victim off with a story concerning the spirits. When he has worked the swindle a few times he will move on to another district before things get too hot for him. It is an old game, but very difficult for the police to make an arrest of the fraudster, let alone prove theft by intent. However, I intend to investigate this Ahmed Bey and nail him once and for all. Are you available for such an enterprise, Watson, over the next few days?'

Whenever Holmes asked me this question I was nearly always able to agree to assist even if it meant a complicated rearrangement of appointments already made. However, to my sorrow, I was unable to manipulate my affairs in that way upon this particular occasion. He took it well, saying, 'Watson, you cannot always be expected to rearrange your life for my benefit. However, I would ask that you try very hard to be here a week from tonight when I again interview Mrs Moran.' I promised that I would do my level best to be present.

During the next seven days I called in once or twice at 221b only to find Holmes absent. Mrs Hudson told me, 'He's been up to his old theatrics again, Doctor; doin' himself up as an old man in a morning coat and white hair and whiskers. The first time I saw him like it I thought he was an intruder — it gave me quite a turn it did!'

I was to see Holmes in his disguise when I arrived at Baker Street at the appointed time and date. To be more exact I was to see him removing his disguise in front of his dressing mirror. He said, 'I have for the better part of the last seven days been Erasmus Barker, an eccentric but wealthy widower. After attending a couple of meetings run by Ahmed Bey I was promoted to become one of the chosen few, allowed to bury and double in value first a gold sovereign and later a five-pound banknote. I knew from experience that whatever was next buried would disappear. However, I made it known to him that if the fifty pounds that I buried was increased I might invest a good part of my savings. I took a chance, Watson, but it worked. Today I dug up a hundred pounds instead of the fifty I had placed in the handkerchief. His greed had made him throw caution to the winds and alter his normal pattern. I imagine Mrs Moran will be delighted with the news and if my ears do not deceive me, here she is!'

My friend had completed his transformation back from the aged eccentric to the ascetic investigator by the time Mrs Hudson ushered her into the room. Anxiety showed in her face as we seated her and offered her refreshment. 'Mr Holmes, I am in such trouble, for all my friends who helped to contribute that fifty pounds are expressing a wish to be reimbursed. Without news from you I have no way to reassure them.'

Holmes raised his eyebrows. 'It is good news, Mrs Moran. By manipulating Ahmed Bey, much as he evidently manipulated you, I have managed to recover your money.' He produced and opened the handkerchief and extracted fifty pounds in notes and handed them to her. 'So you see all is well and you can return the money to your friends.'

She gratefully accepted the money and placed it in her handbag. Then, rather to my surprise she said, 'Grateful as I am, Mr Holmes, I still don't know which way to turn. I can see the workhouse beckoning me. By the time I have paid your fee I'll wager I will again be out of pocket.'

Of course I have always known that Holmes had a kindly side to his nature despite his seeming lack of emotion. But even so he quite surprised and, nay, touched me when he said, 'My dear lady, perhaps you had better take the other fifty pounds that are in the kerchief, at least until you are in a better financial state. Oh, pray do not upset yourself. My fee, needless to say, is omitted entirely.'

Mrs Moran left, repeatedly thanking Holmes for his great generosity. As soon as she was out of earshot I warmly shook my friend by the hand, rather I think to his surprise. I said, 'Holmes I have always held you in great esteem and known that you had a very generous side to your nature. However, what you have done for that poor woman is beyond all expectation. God bless you, my friend!'

Holmes shrugged and said, 'It will all come back, Watson, it will all come back!' I thought I knew the drift of the thought which prompted his remark, 'You mean we all reap what we sow?'

Then he surprised me by saying, 'No, I mean that in a few minutes the money I risked will come back to me.'

I was about to ask for clarification of his words but for an interruption in the shape of a visit from Inspector Lestrade of Scotland Yard. The inspector dropped some bank notes onto the table, 'There you are, Mr Holmes, there is your outlay. The rest of the money I am now holding as evidence — the marked notes, I mean. Forgive me if I depart now but I have to supervise this Mrs Moran — as she calls herself — being charged with complicity in the fraud. The Streatham police have arrested Ahmed Bey. Many thanks for your help. You will of course be needed to give evidence against the wretched pair. Romany fortune tellers used to work the swindle and we at the Yard call it the gypsy switch, but this Ahmed Bey has got a rather more involved system and has been playing for higher stakes.'

I slumped back in my chair, exhausted by trying to grasp the whole situation. At last I recovered enough to ask, 'Do my ears deceive me or did Lestrade say that he had arrested Mrs Moran as a fraud's accomplice? Please explain it all to me, Holmes, for I fear I am confused.'

Sherlock Holmes seated himself comfortably and filled his favourite clay. In his own time, after he had lit the pipe, he began, 'Mrs Moran, actually the wife of Ahmed Bey, presented herself to us as the victim but was in fact Bey's accomplice in a widening of the system which Lestrade has called the gypsy switch. Their idea was not to rely upon people with money showing up at a meeting but to deliberately involve well-known people, sure to have a certain amount of money.'

I gasped, 'They had a nerve to involve you, Holmes, considering your reputation.'

He smiled, 'I think Bey felt that I presented him with a

challenge, and designed a double bluff but when my disguised widower showed up, wealthy and eccentric, all thoughts of Sherlock Holmes went out of the window. Mrs Moran kept the appointment however, not to raise suspicion.'

I asked, 'Where did Lestrade come into the picture?'

He answered, 'Almost from the start, I enlisted his aid, also that of the local bank where Bey conducted business. Marked notes were issued to him.'

I eventually started to see the whole scenario, yet one thing troubled me still. 'Holmes, all of this makes perfect sense, save at what point did you become suspicious of Mrs Moran or rather Mrs Bey?'

He chuckled, 'Her acting ability was more than considerable, but her necklace was not in character. How often have you seen a widow of the class from which she claimed to belong wearing such a necklace — especially one with Egyptian charms on it?'

Ahmed Bey and his wife were charged and both received prison terms. Moreover, in order to reduce those terms of incarceration, they volunteered to restore monies to some of their most recent victims. One or two of the real widows got their money back, thanks to Sherlock Holmes.

The Gantry Point Wreckers

'My dear Watson, I have a most excellent memory and yet I do not recall this episode with wreckers in Gantry Point. When do you suggest that it occurred?'

I was at the old rooms in Baker Street which I had shared at various portions of the most formative parts of my life with my friend, Sherlock Holmes. The visit was the first I had paid him in some months and I found him crusty and yet amiable as only he could blend these characteristics. I had brought with me the outline of a manuscript which I had been thinking of sending to the *Strand Magazine*. As ever, I needed to get the blessing of the world's greatest consulting detective before doing so. I had tentatively titled it *The Gantry Point Wreckers* and Holmes had studied it carefully with some bewilderment appearing to grow in his facial expression.

He repeated, 'When, Watson, do you claim that this episode happened?'

It took me a minute or so to be able to answer his question truthfully for at first I could not remember if it was the last winter of the nineteenth century or the first of the twentieth. At last accuracy returned to my mind because it had been in 1899 that Holmes's doctor had advised an immediate break from the regime which had caused a serious nervous breakdown. I have never made known to my readers quite how serious that breakdown was, although the hints have been there in my writings of the cases that led up to the problem; the narcotics, lack of natural sleep and the merciless regime of hard work both physical and mental. In fact his doctor had said, 'Take your friend to the coast and give him several daily doses of this medication.'

I had studied the medicine bottle and, whilst a medical man myself, I rather blanched at the thought of that particular remedy in large regular doses. The doctor was a specialist in the maladies of the mind.

Bideford in North Devon was the little white town which I selected for Holmes's recuperation. It was a delightful place, of the kind which no criminal beyond the odd poacher was likely to frequent. The Bridge Hotel was comfortable and adjacent to the age-old wooden bridge after which it was named. Holmes took the autumnal gales and rains in his stride as he stood upon that fine old bridge, sometimes for twenty minutes at a time, motionless as if scanning the waters for some particular expected craft. The strong opiate was doing its work, making him seem to be none too deeply concerned for anything. His appetite began to return and I felt that a few weeks in this environment would work wonders for him. But it was odd to see Sherlock Holmes so lax, not seeming to crave either excitement or cocaine.

Then one morning things were to change somewhat for the hotel, and its surroundings were to buzz with the discussion of a local topic, that of shipwrecks in general and the wreck of the *Coriander* in particular. Holmes picked up the general buzz of conversation, despite his lethargy, and for the first time since we had left the metropolis demanded to see a newspaper. The one which was brought to him at the breakfast table was of the local variety, *The Bideford and Barnstaple Budget.* Its front page was filled with the news of the *Coriander* and its sinking through being thrown onto the rocks. Perhaps that which interested Holmes the more was the fact that much of its cargo of valuable cordial and timbers, bullion and other valuables had been washed up on the shore ready to be claimed as treasure-trove or, in many cases, doubtless to vanish without trace.

At first I thought that my friend was taking the most passing interest in this news; indeed I hoped that this was so. But my hopes were dashed when he said, 'Come, Watson, it is a splendid day despite the gusting wind, or perhaps on account of it, so let us take ourselves to Gantry Point for a change of scene.' My heart sank, for Gantry Point was the very site of the wrecking of the *Coriander* and many another brave ship according to the local news sheet.

Gantry Point proved to be a village built, rather as is the better known Clovelly, upon a series of steps or stages with a dwelling at the cliff. It has a single street of steps, each step with a dwelling at each side of it. It was picturesque, especially the Lobster Pot which was an old smugglers' inn almost at the Point itself. We sipped a local brew known as tanglefoot from great tankards and tried to converse with the locals. However, most of these fell silent at the sight of us and muttered to each other regarding 'furriners.'

Eventually one or two of these fisher folk and sailors

allowed us to buy them cider and accepted a fill of tobacco from Holmes's copious pouch. One fellow, with ear rings and a fully rigged schooner tattooed upon his forearm actually unbent so far as to exchange a word or two with us. He seemed relieved when I explained that my friend was a recuperating invalid, and I feel sure that none of them recognised him as Sherlock Holmes the great detective. Indeed Holmes introduced himself as Septimus Eagle, and dubbed me as Professor Warrender.

Our new acquaintance excused himself and rejoined his friends. Although I could not hear their talk I surmised that he was reassuring them concerning us. Then they went into a very close confab indeed and looked so conspiratorial that I would have dearly loved to have heard what they were saying. As for Holmes, my worst fears were realised when I decided that medication or no, his mind was involving itself with the wreckers, and that his suspicions were aroused.

Then a young lad entered the public house; he was probably in his twenties, though from the innocence of his expression and clumsy childlike walk seemed much younger than that. By the way he was treated, made a mock of and buffeted around it became clear that he was the traditional village idiot. Later he came over to us and studied us carefully as infants are inclined to do. Then he pointed at Holmes and seemed to be trying to say something. However, it was impossible to understand him so I simply smiled and nodded. Holmes offered him some tobacco but he made a gesture of disgust. Eventually he rejoined those who obviously despised him, continuing their converse as if he were not there.

The crowd of roughnecks eventually left the establishment and the youngster remained, seated alone and staring into space. His reverie was interrupted by the appearance of the local police sergeant, who nodded to us and waved to the boy. He said, 'Don't let poor daft Davey fret you gennlemen, he be 'mazed ee be!' We quietly discussed with him the matter of the wrecker's activities and his honest ruddy face grew serious. 'Can't handle it gents, I'd need a detective force to do that. You see they operate from various likely places, luring the ships with a lamp, hoping they will mistake it for a lighthouse. At this time of the year the gales are strong enough most nights for them to operate profitably. We don't even know the names or origins of the ships that they are after. They know what will pass near here, they have a sort of secret service in that direction. So far we have never managed to be on the right spot at the right time. Now that young Davey could tell us a lot that would help, if only he could speak, or even understand what was going on around him, for the poor lad is a complete idiot so they talks freely in front of him. Oh, I've tried to get sense from him but it is no good. Well, good day to you gents!' He nodded and crossed to the bar for his cider.

I tried to change the subject whenever Holmes touched on it but I could see that he was more than interested in becoming involved in catching the wreckers. He said as much, if not in as many words, as we climbed the giant stepping stones of the street. On our left we saw what at first glance appeared to be a collection of children's toys inside a ground-floor sash window of one of the houses. However when we looked more closely we could see that they were objects of a more involved nature. Models rather than toys; beautifully carved sailing ships with their flags and rigging. Also there were figures of sailors and fishermen some even in pirate raiment. Holmes found these fascinating, especially when the unfortunate lad, Davey, appeared in the window, grimacing and holding a knife and a piece of driftwood which he was in the act of carving. Holmes gasped, 'Upon my word, a brain and a skill hide behind that mask of imbecility, Watson! See how skilled and detailed those models are.'

I wanted to purchase some items from the village shop which was opposite that model display. Holmes did not accompany me into the shop, but when I emerged I could see him conversing with a middle-aged lady in the doorway of the house. Davey leered and waved in the background.

Thereafter Holmes insisted on visiting the village at Gantry Point daily, and always he would linger in front of Davey's window to admire the ever-changing display. 'His mother is a tower of strength, Watson, but even she cannot accurately communicate with him. It is a tragedy. He cannot read or write but enjoys looking at old magazines which have illustrations.' I looked sadly at the latest examples of Davey's work; a ship, full-masted and bearing the French tricolour, and some pirates which had been arranged upon a model hillock, fashioned from stones and turf. It was a passable likeness of the Gantry Point after which the village had been named.

'Upon my word!' Holmes sprang into something like his old manner. 'Who says, Watson, that he cannot communicate?'

We spent an uncomfortable evening in hiding behind some rocks near the point itself. The police sergeant had, after consultation with Holmes, rounded up a few trusted cronies who were in hiding with us. As the gale grew in its intensity we were chilled to the bone, as we watched for activity. At about midnight the wreckers appeared with a lamp which they placed upon the highest rock of the point. Their target ship eventually came into view but just as they turned on their deadly luring lamp one of the policeman's companions leapt up with a signal lamp and began to warn off the French vessel before it could be dashed onto the rocks. As for the sergeant himself, he had the proof he needed and grabbed at the holder of the deadly light. His friends aided him to capture the four men who were gathered in the shadows around the principal wrongdoer.

I'm happy to say that there was no fight, the wreckers being sensible enough to accept when they were beaten. The man who had spoken to us in the public house glared at us and said 'All right, who spilled his guts to you? Tell me and I'll spill them for good!'

Later we sat in the police sergeant's cottage drinking steaming tea and eating bread and cheese which the police wife was good enough to furnish us with. 'How did you manage to get Davey to tell you all that, Mr Holmes, for no one else has been able to get a peep out of him.'

Holmes explained, 'When I saw his models in the window I realised that a considerable mind was trapped in the shell of an idiot. When you were in the shop, Watson, I spoke to him and his mother. Evidently the lad had recognised me from Paget's drawings in the *Strand*. I realised that he understood what was said to him and I arranged with him to leave a message in his window by way of his models concerning the next wrecking that he learned of. He deserves a medal for his part in this business.'

Davey got no medal but settled for a handshake from Sherlock Holmes and a supply of sophisticated carving knives.

As I finished reminding Holmes of the episode he said, 'Watson, that wretched medicine which you connived to dose me with made me forget almost everything which happened during that incident. If your story is true — and I question it a little — it must have been the episode itself which jolted me back into normality rather than the medication.'

The South Downs Railway Mystery

'Just down your street, Mr Holmes, a mystery concerning an enigmatic written message and some numbers written upon the back of a postal card.'

Inspector Lestrade dropped the postcard onto the breakfast table of my friend Mr Sherlock Holmes. He was an early visitor although the breakfast had been dealt with and cleared away by the bustling Mrs Hudson. Holmes poured some steaming coffee into an extra cup, which the good lady had thoughtfully supplied, and passed it to our colleague, saying, 'Suppose you tell us the whole story, my dear Lestrade, before you tax me with the message on the postcard. It is early, early enough so that caffeine and nicotine have not yet sent their tiny darts into my grey matter; at least not to the required degree.'

Lestrade grunted, 'It is nine and forty, with half the day gone already, but then I know you have strange habits. As you suggest I will start at the beginning. We have in custody a certain Ronald Carstairs, suspected of having taken the Carradine jewels, the theft of which you are doubtless aware.'

Holmes nodded. 'Of course, and I am also familiar with the background of safecracker Carstairs. You are reasonably certain that you have your right man?'

Lestrade took out his cigarette case and as it was filled with Turkish cigarettes we forsook our pipes for once and we each accepted one. Lestrade lit a vesta from which he and Holmes lit up, leaving me to find my own matches. This was not through any kind of thoughtlessness upon Lestrade's part; he knew that I observed the army superstition concerning three from one match. He replied to Holmes's question, 'Reasonably certain? Why, I am positively so! Not only did the job have all the hallmarks of his style but he could not account for his movements for the time in question. All we can do is hold him for a few days more until we can hopefully prove something against him. I have bullied and pleaded in turn but he will say nothing. There is no loot to be found at his address but he was about to post the card when we arrested him. We believe, my colleagues and I, that the message on the card refers, possibly through a code, to the place where the jewels are secreted.'

At length Holmes studied the card, then asked, 'Has Carstairs made comment upon the card?'

Lestrade replied, 'Says that it is just a message to a friend concerning a bet on a horse race. We are also holding the man to whom the card is addressed but, as you can imagine, we will be able to hold him for an even shorter period than we can Carstairs.'

Holmes remarked, 'Take care, Lestrade, that you keep both of them apart in case the message should be given verbally and the second man slips through your fingers.'

The inspector grunted, 'We are not quite idiots you know, that's why we are holding them in different institutions.'

Holmes nodded, 'Quite so, most wise.'

I considered it tactful to interrupt at this point, 'May I see the card, Holmes?'

My friend passed the card to me. 'Make of it what you can, my dear Watson, for I will value your comments.' I examined the card carefully taking my time on this. On one side it had a depiction of some donkeys on the beach with the words Fun at Margate superimposed upon the seascape at the rear. On the reverse were the usual two divisions; one for a message and the other for the name and address of the person to whom the card was to be sent. There was a faint mark from a rubber stamp in the corner of the back of the card; with the aid of Holmes's lens I made out the words Rathbones Tavistock Street. The message area bore the words, written, or rather printed by pen with violet ink, SDR 17393. UNDER CUSHION HARD.

After some thought I said, 'The card was purchased from a shop, Rathbones, which is evidently in Tavistock Street in Margate, some years ago, for it is considerably faded. As for the message, well the letters SDR and the numbers possibly refer to some kind of left luggage or poste restante arrangement. There is the reference to something being under the cushion and hard. I think there may be some jeweller's display cushions in a deposit box, some soft and one hard. The latter perhaps secretes the jewels? The address to which the card was to be sent is within the London area, but I imagine the deposit box is in Margate. Carstairs possibly bought the card when there to deposit the jewels.'

As I placed the card back to its place before Holmes on the table the detective clapped his hands languidly in mock applause. I assumed he meant that some vital clue, obvious to him, had eluded me, and asked him if this was so.

He smiled mockingly as he said, 'My dear Watson, you really surpass yourself. No, you have not missed any particular obvious sign, you have seen everything yet understood nothing.'

Lestrade, for once, leapt to my defence, 'Come, Mr Holmes, the doctor has made a lot of sense to my mind.'

Holmes looked at us each in turn with mockery, then softened at least in his speech as he said, 'Come, gentlemen. What you have both said would be spoken by most men of intellect. I, however, am not a man of intellect alone, for I have dedicated my life, as you know, to a study of reading the more obscure from the obvious. Let me take your first point, Watson; Rathbones, far from being a seaside emporium is one for postcard collectors in Tavistock Street, which is just off the Strand. This fact explains its faded condition and has no bearing on when it was purchased. Now the letters and numbers. Well, SDR could well refer to SOUTH DOWNS RAILWAY and the number could be that of a carriage, being one of a great many which are used upon that line.

'We are indeed looking for a safe-deposit arrangement, albeit an unofficial one. The seat cushions in the carriage are possibly those referred to, so at least, Watson, you are doubtless right in thinking that the loot is stowed inside a cushion. However, the word hard I feel does not refer to the firmness of padding, but rather to a beach or piece of firm ground near to water; which is often called a hard. I do not as yet understand the connection however. So, Inspector, I suggest that you make haste in tracing the carriage owned by the South Downs Railway which bears the number 17393.'

The logic expressed by his words could not be denied, and Lestrade departed post-haste to make such enquiry.

It was only a few hours later that we saw Lestrade again, for he returned at about four in the afternoon with some interesting news. 'You were right, Holmes, the South Downs Railway indeed had a carriage with that number. But unfortunately they no longer own it. You see, every year or two they dispose of their oldest carriages. That bearing number 17393 was one of those disposed of in this way, quite recently. The sale was made evidently at Brighton, in a storage area next to the railway.'

Holmes consulted his hunter. 'A little late for action today, Lestrade, but early in the morning the game is definitely afoot!'

On the following morning the three of us found ourselves standing in a large glassed railway shed where numerous elderly carriages stood. The superintendent of sales consulted his record for us and traced the number of the carriage we were seeking. 'Sold to a covey from Johnson's Hard, which is at Shoreham.' I knew that little town well which was west of Brighton, just short of Worthing. Not much more than a fishing village really, we were standing in its high street within the hour thanks to the police gig commandeered by Lestrade.

The shore ran along behind the south high street buildings, but it was an estuary rather than a sea shore, for the latter was beyond an island of shale and sand about a quarter of a mile betwixt us and the English Channel. Ferry boats plied their trade in carrying folk to that island, upon which quite a number of rather undistinguished buildings could be vaguely seen. We found a local who told us that we were standing on Dolphin Hard, but that it was more often known as Johnson's Hard as there was a Johnson, a joiner, with premises there.

Mr Johnson, the joiner, we soon found in a timber building where wooden lengths were stored. He had the speech of a southern Englishman, of a generation as yet unaffected by the contamination of London argot. 'He worked y'ere masters, this Carstairs worked y'ere, on them noo bungalows we built on the beach!' He pointed with some drama toward the hastily built structures in the distance. 'Not our best work, but down to a price, good sirs, cobbled together with railway carriages and that!'

We took the ferry boat to Bungalow Town, as the island was called locally. It did not take us long to locate the rickety building recently fashioned by Johnson. There were two railway carriages which formed the sides of the building and a gabled roof which connected them. Far from beautiful it was yet ingenious in its construction, with back and front entrance doors built at each of its open ends. Doubtless the carriages were for use as bedrooms with a living area between. This proved in fact to be so, as we learned upon gaining access to the house where a recently arrived owner showed the inspector around the building. He said, 'Only just moved in, Inspector. Place is a shambles but look at anything you want to.' There were packing cases everywhere but we soon found what we were seeking, through a bedroom door marked SDR 17393.

We lifted the cushions in turn, the second revealing a hessian bag which in fact contained the missing gems! The owner looked at our find with interest, 'Well I never, old Johnson said it was a bargain too!'

Back at Baker Street we partook of a tasty meal and discussed the case of the South Downs Railway carriage.

Holmes said, 'Lestrade has the evidence he needs to convict Carstairs at least, and Lady Carradine has her diamonds back.'

As for Sherlock Holmes, well, he participated on his own without intent to do more than help a friend. But I am happy to say that a letter bearing a crest which contained a generous cheque found its way to 221b within days. Holmes looked at it and said to me, 'Watson, I never vary my fee as a rule but, as I was not engaged by the good lady in the first place, we can take ourselves off to Simpsons for a slap-up meal with clear consciences!'

The Case of the Flying Messengers

Throughout the Baker Street years (as I have latterly taken to calling my halcyon days) my friend Sherlock Holmes conducted a strange relationship with those who operated from an official position regarding the detection of crime; Scotland Yard in general and Inspector Lestrade in particular. Both men having devoted so much of their lives to the enigma of crime had really only that much in common; as men being as unlike as chalk is from cheese. Holmes went about his work completely uncluttered by routine or preconceived ideas, whereas Lestrade was up to his neck in ritual and procedure.

This is not to suggest that Lestrade was lacking in intellect or even in a certain brilliance but Holmes's mind operated on quite a different plane. Uncluttered by mundane assumption he had a super intellect which could be directed wherever he required it to be directed. The Lestrades of this world are essential, for when a crime has been solved someone has to operate the cleansing process which will tidy up the whole scenario and bring down the curtain to applause which some might feel more deserved by the producer than by the star. Sherlock Holmes, the miracle worker, so often had to remain in the wings whilst Lestrade, the actor-manager took the bows. In these chronicles concerning the adventures of my friend, which it has long been my pleasure to document, I have given many examples of this, yet no example could be more typical than the enigma of the flying messengers.

The old Queen was still upon the throne, if fading fast, when Lestrade called upon us with this particular problem. We knew that he brought one because he hardly ever made social calls. The inspector had by that time a great respect for the talents of my friend which he appeared loath to express. Pleasantries over he smirked as he said, 'I have an interesting little puzzle which I am sure will soon be resolved but that I think might interest you.'

Holmes's eyes twinkled as he said, 'Come, Inspector, the solution of puzzles is food and drink to us both. Often before you have brought me an enigma at a time when I have been bored to distraction with everything around me. Once or twice, I believe, I have even been able to be of help to you, have I not?'

Lestrade grunted as he brushed his moustache with his fingers, 'I seem to remember that you have sometimes been able to make that suggestion which has set me on the right road to solving a case, Mr Holmes.' I managed to turn a snigger into an asthmatic wheeze.

Lestrade then told his story. 'You know we often get asked to assist the customs and excise people whose work is by no means as run of the mill as might be imagined. Sometimes they find it diplomatic to let a suspect slip through their nets in order to catch the receiver as well as the smuggler. You know the sort of thing? The smuggler thinks he has got away with it and catches a train from Dover to Charing Cross there to meet some shady character ready to exchange banknotes for watches or brandy. Where the meeting is obviously an arranged one our people, in plain clothes, are able to pounce. 'Tis run of the mill and we handle such cases all the time, but sometimes the customs people come to us with a belief that an evasion is being made and yet no real proof is involved.'

I felt bound to ask, 'Could it not be that sometimes no crime exists?'

He nodded, 'One must go softly for that reason, but this affair of the pigeons is senseless enough to shout of criminal activity!'

Holmes was intrigued now and charged his clay with the Scottish mixture, as he asked, 'Why don't you tell us the whole story, Lestrade? Come we promise not to laugh at any obvious lack of evil.'

Lestrade grunted and then took a deep breath before launching himself upon a rather confused narration. 'Not far from Dover there dwells a gentleman who keeps pigeons of the homing variety. So far nothing unusual. Now in Calais there dwells another gentleman who is also a pigeon-fancier. The Englishman regularly releases a flock of pigeons which fly to Calais and the Frenchman releases a flock which return to their home loft in Dover.'

Holmes interjected, 'I assume that the pigeons are returned to the places from which they flew by ferry boat?'

Lestrade nodded, 'Exactly and, so far, there is nothing unusual save in the quite large numbers of birds involved. At first we assumed that they were being raced, but this could surely not happen with such great regularity?'

I stated the obvious, 'Pigeons are often used to carry messages, usually in a small container, strapped to a leg.'

Holmes said, 'Good point, Watson, but tell me Lestrade, just how many pigeons are flown at any one time?'

The policeman said, 'A score, sometimes more.'

Holmes frowned, 'Cuts out the message theory surely. What are your own suspicions, Lestrade?'

The inspector replied, 'We thought perhaps that diamonds were being smuggled in the message containers which are indeed present on the birds' legs.'

Holmes asked, 'Has any attempt been made to investigate such a theory?'

'Yes, visits were made jointly to both suspect lofts in collaboration with the *sûreté* but only messages were found in the containers.'

Holmes was interested now. 'What form did these messages take?'

Lestrade explained, 'Just simple little phrases like, "Another flight on Friday". Our cipher people tried to make more of this than I suspect is there.'

Sherlock Holmes looked thoughtful and re-lit his pipe with a vesta. 'How many of the birds did you examine?'

Lestrade shrugged. 'Perhaps a quarter of the birds concerned. With no obvious law breaking involved we are not entitled to accuse or even investigate too openly.'

Holmes agreed, 'Both fanciers could merely be eccentrics indulging in some regular race. Yet, I doubt it, my dear Lestrade, I doubt it!'

The inspector looked almost relieved to hear even a hint at the possibility of wrongdoing from the world's first consulting detective. 'You think I did right to draw your attention to the matter then?'

Holmes replied, 'Most certainly, Inspector. I am intrigued,

and if you can ascertain when you think the next movement of pigeons is due I will try to give your enigma my undivided attention.'

Lestrade looked relieved and said, 'Observation of regular routine tells us that the next flock of French pigeons will arrive at Dover at seven of the clock this very evening.'

So it came about that the three of us found ourselves upon the South Downs at about six and thirty, stationed among some gorse although there was very little chance of our being overlooked save by a few sheep.

Holmes had brought with him a strange package which proved, as I had suspected, to contain a weapon. It was, however, an unusual firing piece being a form of air rifle of no great power. 'You see, Lestrade, I wish to bring down at least one of the carriers without drawing attention to the fact that I am doing so. I am not a sporting shot as you well know, but a good enough marksman none the less.' (I secretly thought of poor Mrs Hudson's wall with its V.R. of bullets!) 'Whilst we await the avian flock, Lestrade, I wish you would give me some idea of the type of man we are dealing with. I refer to the English fancier.'

Lestrade recited as if reading from an invisible notebook. 'The man under observation is a Geoffrey Carter, well built and about thirty years of age. Evidently of independent means he seems seldom to leave his home which is quite impressive, set apart from the village of Gorsehill, quite near to this very spot. He appears, from our observations, to be quite absorbed with his pigeon loft.'

If the reader has no shooting interest he might be innocent concerning the sounds made by a flock of birds flying low. Mother nature has, I assure you, produced few sounds more pleasing. We heard the flutter, softly at first then more intrusive as the pigeons came into view. Holmes cocked the air rifle, raised it, took aim and fired. There was practically no noise, yet one of the birds seemed to cease movement in mid-air, then fell rather in the manner of a shuttlecock. This slow descent enabled us to realise just where it would end up. As well for we had no retrieving spaniel!

Holmes located his bird among the gorse without much difficulty and held it aloft. 'You see, my eye has lost little of its cunning. Now, Inspector, we will repair to your local police station in order to examine our prize. I will not, I think, essay a second shot. After all, our suspect might attach little notice to the loss of a single bird putting it down to an attack by a hawk or even a small boy with a weapon such as mine. More than one could alert his suspicions.'

We regained the lane where a police gig awaited us. The constable touched his helmet and awoke the drowsing horse. We were soon in the back room of his cottage; the nearest thing to a police station that Gorsehill could boast. Lestrade treated Reynolds just as one would expect a police inspector to treat a lowly underling, but Holmes spoke to him as one would normally address one's host. 'My dear Reynolds, do you think you could clear your kitchen table so that we could use it for our operations?' The good-natured constable took some food and utensils from the scrubbed wooden table top so that we could lay the dead pigeon thereon.

To me it was just an extremely dead pigeon but Holmes waxed almost poetic over it. 'You see before you, gentlemen, one of nature's wonders; the *columbidae* or domesticated rock dove. It can be bred and trained to return to its home loft from wherever it is taken. I believe the Romans brought it here in the form of a large fan-tailed dove, to feed their armies. From this original a great many sub-species of pigeon have been evolved. You will notice that the beautiful creature, which against my nature I have been required to destroy, carries a message in a container fixed to its leg.' I was all for opening the container and examining the message, but Holmes dwelt lovingly upon the bird and its plumage. He lifted its wing, saying, 'Observe the beauty of the feathering which no artist could possibly do justice to, or match its beauty of design.' Lestrade coughed with impatience and I confess I was beginning to be irritated by Holmes's dalliance.

At last my friend appeared to be reaching the climax of his oration. 'Inspector, from what you have told me it seems that the message itself will tell us little. However, for the sake of thoroughness we will examine it.' He withdrew the slip of paper from the cylinder and read the message aloud, 'The Frenchman in the onion patch will be delighted.'

Lestrade turned to Reynolds, 'Do you know of a foreigner around here who runs a market garden?'

The Constable shook his head, 'No, sir!'

Holmes chuckled, 'I do not think that it is quite that simple, Inspector. Now let us examine the cartridge itself.'

Lestrade grunted, 'Surely it is the message within that concerns us?'

Holmes, seeming to ignore the Yard man, unscrewed the cartridge and removed it from the bird's leg. He scanned the cylinder itself through his glass. His eyes narrowed like the iris of a camera lens being stopped down for added focus. Then he handed both glass and metal tube to Lestrade. 'What do you make of it, Inspector?'

Lestrade examined the article keenly and then said, 'It is of grey metal and appears to have been in contact with some article treated with gold leaf — judging by the minute flecks of gold on the surface.'

When my turn for examination came I was at first tempted toward the same conclusion. However, I then spotted something unusual. 'There is a droplet, though minute, at the end of the tube, of grey paint.'

Holmes nodded, 'Well spotted, Watson, there are no gold flecks. Rather do we see a gold-coloured tube, painted over with grey.'

The inspector snorted, 'Why would anyone want to do that?'

I volunteered, 'To prevent the light upon the bright metal attracting hawks when catching the sunlight?'

Holmes considered, 'A good thought, but I think I have a better one. I believe that the canister may be fashioned from precious metal and then disguised.' We gasped as Holmes scraped away some grey paint with his penknife to reveal a golden glint below.

Lestrade whistled, 'I see it all now. The Frenchman is sending these cylinders of pure gold, painted over to look like the common or garden object. I will see to it that both fanciers involved are arrested, at least on suspicion of customs evasion!'

There was an air of finality in Lestrade's words which prompted Holmes to ask, 'What about the French dealer in gold at Hatton Garden? Eh?' Lestrade was bewildered.

I dared to enquire, 'You mean that the onion patch could refer to Hatton Garden, which is a likely area for a dealer in gold?'

Holmes said, 'Exactly. The French fancier not only sends gold but suggests to whom it should be offered.'

A few days later Lestrade again called upon us at Baker Street to tell us that his case had been resolved. 'We arrested both fanciers with the co-operation of the *sûreté* and it was just as we suspected with a certain Legrand — a Hatton Garden dealer — also involved and apprehended. It was a lucky thought from Doctor Watson which made it possible for me to solve the case!'

After the inspector had departed it was some considerable time before I dared address Holmes or even catch his eye. Indeed it was poor Mrs Hudson who eventually caused an explosion of his wrath when she served our dinner — a brace of plump wood pigeon!

Sherlock Holmes and a Fraud in Baker Street

'Holmes, just take a look at this!' I threw before my friend Mr Sherlock Holmes a copy of a cheaply printed journal with a garish cover illustration depicting a lean-faced man in a pink dressing robe inspecting a document with the aid of a lens. Above the illustration there was a headline which declared, Ruxton Lake Investigates! Below the picture there appeared the words, Read the thrilling exploits of the famous Baker Street Detective!

Holmes chuckled and said, 'The sincerest form of flattery, my dear Watson.'

I should perhaps explain to the reader that the events of which I write happened many years ago, quite shortly after the appearance in the *Strand Magazine* of my first few chronicles concerning the exploits of my friend. The initial instalments had been popular enough, but by the time of the third or fourth episode they had gained a popularity for which neither Holmes, or I had been prepared. The public imagination had been captured by *The Adventures of Sherlock Holmes* to the extent that lines of people would appear at the newspaper shops on the day that each new issue was published.

Of course I had always been vaguely aware that plagiarism

of the written word was common enough. But the effect that it would have upon a poor wronged author was something I had not realised until it affected me. I had been taking a stroll in Baker Street when I had wandered into the newsagents to see if the new issue of the *Strand* had appeared when my eyes alighted upon this cheaply printed journal, *Crimes of the Week*. Its cover I have already described but I should explain that the Ruxton Lake adventure within was titled *The case of the dotted bandanna*, and I was soon to discover that it was a colourable imitation of a manuscript of mine titled *The Speckled Band*. The names of the characters had been changed and there were quite a few other changes of location and detail but it remained a clumsily written imitation of my work.

All of this would have been irritating enough but there remained another, more serious aspect to the business; the episode which had been copied was one which had not yet appeared in print in the *Strand*. My blood ran cold at the thought that my readers might think that I had imitated this ill-written rubbish. I remarked as much to Holmes as he glanced through *Crimes of the Week*.

'My dear fellow, pray do not distress yourself. When *The Speckled Band* appears in print any reader of intellect will recognise its authenticity of style and content.'

He meant well but his words failed to calm my anxiety. I said, 'You were right, Holmes, when you disapproved of my writing accounts of your exploits. See where it has got me. The author, if such he can be called, has even situated his character in Baker Street.'

Holmes continued to take a becalming attitude toward me, 'At least there is no Doctor Watson, or even a medical man of similar name; rather does he appear to be assisted

by a schoolboy called Pinkerton and a bloodhound, Bruno.'
When I asked Holmes if he thought I could take legal
action he shook his head, 'No, Watson, the only aspect
which might be construed as unlawful is the anticipation of
your work. Not content with plagiarising your published
work the author has gained knowledge of your episodes
which are yet to appear.'

I called, that very afternoon, at the offices of the Com-
bined Press, publishers of the offensive journal. These were
in Fleet Street, at the top of a dingy building, and by the
time I had climbed the several flights of mouldering stairs
my temper had reached boiling point. 'Where is Edwin
Carstairs, author of the Ruxton Lake rubbish?'

Nobody knew but I was ushered into the presence of
the editor of *Crime of the Week*. He proved to be a rather
seedy looking man, sitting behind an overstocked desk in
his shirt sleeves. What he lacked in charm of manner he
seemed to be trying to make up for with energy and
appeared to believe in the old adage the best way to de-
fend is to attack. He answered my complaints with a spir-
ited offensive, 'I would point out, Doctor Watson, that
our paper, one of several that I edit, appeals to a very
different public to the readership of the *Strand*. Our readers may be younger and less well educated but they are
more numerous and they are the salt of the earth. Your
colleague, Holmes, should be flattered to think that they
will assume, even if wrongly, that he is the great Ruxton
Lake. The reason that you cannot see Edwin Carstairs is
because no such author exists. I have some half a dozen or
more jobbing writers who contribute Ruxton Lake stories,
all of them published under that *nom de plume*.

'As for your accusation that your manuscripts have been tampered with, I can only suggest that this so-called similarity of characters and plot is a figment of your imagination. Even were you to produce this famous manuscript I would have no guarantee that you had not colluded with the editor of the *Strand* and copied one of our *Crimes of the Week.*'

Over muffins and tea back at Baker Street I conveyed to Holmes something of my encounter with the editor of the offending weekly paper. He had taken the opportunity afforded by my absence to read the story carefully. He said, 'This Ruxton Lake is everything that I should be, Watson! He has my powers of deduction, my energy, but none of my vices. One can hold him up as a paragon of virtue as an example for the young. I don't think you could do that with your humble servant.'

Dutifully I disagreed with him, but secretly felt that his excessive use of narcotics would not go down too well with the parents and teachers of juvenile readers.

The powers that were at the helm of the *Strand* were not in favour of any sort of legal steps being taken. At that time, having no wish to upset their more than conservative readership and not subscribing to Barnum's famous views that any publicity is good, they advised me to ignore the incident and treat *Crime of the Week* with the contempt that they thought it deserved. But I was still worried by the whole episode, mainly concerning how the consortium known as Edwin Carstairs had managed to gain a glimpse at *The Speckled Band* before the editor of the *Strand* had even received it. Of course I had one advantage and one only: Sherlock Holmes.

My friend gave my case his undivided attention. After all, he had a vested interest in it. He said, 'Watson, let us start at the beginning. You work upon your manuscripts at your desk, which has a sophisticated lock which you secure at night. How about your discarded sheets. Are these dropped into the wastebasket?'

I had to confess that which I am loath to admit now to my many readers, saying, 'Holmes, I realise that it is most unprofessional of me but I neither prepare a rough draft nor do I rewrite or correct that which I have written. Sometimes I cross out a word or two and replace them with others written above or in the margin but, due to the fact that I compose each episode in my head based upon those very vivid memories of adventures that we have shared, there is no other written record.'

Holmes was surprised, 'Upon my word, you must be unique among authors in that respect. Very well, we can eliminate all thought of purloined drafts. Your actual manuscript therefore is read and conveyed to the wrong quarter. As I remember, you take the manuscript to the magazine yourself do you not, rather than trusting it to the penny post?'

I replied, rather guiltily, 'I used to do so, but of late I have taken to sending it by messenger.'

Holmes's eyes narrowed, 'Ah, now at last we may be seeing a light; who is the messenger?'

I answered guiltily, 'Why it is our pageboy, Billy.'

Rather to my surprise Holmes did not chastise me, rather saying, 'Well, Watson, I would trust my life to Billy, in fact on occasion I have.' Much relieved I could only concur that Billy was to be trusted in all ways. Holmes said,

'We must talk to Billy at once. He is a shrewd lad and could possibly tell us that which will explain the mystery.'

I rang the bell and when Mrs Hudson appeared I asked her, 'Would you be so kind as to send Billy up to us?' I fancied I noticed a guilty tone when after a minute pause she replied, 'Billy? Oh, why of course, Doctor, I'll send him up at once.'

The familiar figure of Billy the page was soon stood before us, his familiar cherubic face perhaps uncharacteristic in its vaguely furtive expression. Holmes smiled at him reassuringly, 'Ah, Billy my lad, we just wanted to ask you a question or two regarding the manuscripts which you conveyed to Fleet Street for Doctor Watson.'

The page muttered, 'Yessir, you mean those tales for the magazine?'

I blanched a little I think when he used the word tales. Holmes continued to address Billy. 'When did you take the last one?'

He looked puzzled for a minute, then said, 'Not last Tuesday but the one before, I remember we 'ad pancakes in the kitchen.'

I said, 'Jove, yes, it was Shrove Tuesday. I remember that too.'

Holmes glared at me, then asked Billy, 'How did you travel to Fleet Street?'

He said, 'I took 'ansom didn't I, 'cause the doctor said it was not safe to go on the 'orse bus in case it got stole . . . the manuscrip', not the bus!' Holmes and I could neither of us conceal a grin.

Holmes enquired, 'Did you take the first cab on the rank, Billy?'

He nodded, 'Of course I did, I was in 'urry.'

Holmes looked at him keenly, 'Billy, you remember, of course, the inspector from Scotland Yard who has collaborated with me so often?'

He looked furtive, 'Yes sir, what about him?'

Holmes asked, 'What is his name?'

The boy shifted from one foot to the other and eventually said, 'I forget just this minute.'

There was an uncomfortable pause, a silence broken by Holmes's enquiry, 'What is your name, Jimmy, George or Harry? Certainly it is not Billy, or rather not the Billy I know despite a truly remarkable likeness. Billy would never have taken the first cab on the rank under any circumstances any more than he would forget the name of Inspector Lestrade!'

The page hung his head; I could still not believe that he was not our Billy. After what seemed like an age he spoke, 'Bertie 'ain't I? I'm Billy's twin brother Herbert. I come up from the country. Billy's uncle Charlie wanted him to help with his work. I couldn't do it because I can't read like Billy can. Mrs Hudson said it would be alright, just for a month. The doctor gave me this manuscript and I was just about to take it when this bloke comes up and says he would save me a journey and take it and he give me 'arf a crown!'

I was aghast that I had trusted my manuscripts to this young rascal. I would have trusted Billy with my life, but could not have been expected to know that he had a twin brother, aye and at that one without his sense of responsibility.

Holmes smiled grimly and said, 'Well, Watson, until the real Billy returns you must take the trouble to deliver your precious manuscripts in person. We cannot stop *Crime of the Week* lampooning me in the guise of Ruxton Lake, but at least they can be deprived of the use of accounts of my cases. But now, what are we to do with this young impostor?'

Bertie stood before us with a hangdog air which made him look a little less like his cheery band box of a twin brother. At last he spoke, 'Please, Mr 'Olmes, don't send me to chokey, I'll never do such a thing again!'

I felt uncomfortable regarding his fate despite his having caused both Holmes and me such embarrassment. I said, 'Come my lad, bear up, I'm sure there is no need of extreme measures of punishment.'

Holmes said, 'Please depart, Bertie, and send Mrs Hudson up to us; you will be informed later as to our deliberations.'

The housekeeper was apologetic and informed us that the genuine Billy would be returning to his duties within the week. 'I'll send Bertie home with a flea in his ear, sir, and his uncle Charlie won't half give him a fourpenny one!'

I had always suspected a kindly and forgiving side to Holmes's nature, however well disguised it might have been. He said, 'No need for retribution, Mrs Hudson. I believe the unfortunate events of the past days have been a lesson to all concerned.'

Readers of my accounts of the activities of Sherlock Holmes have often been kind enough to inform me that these chronicles have an authentic ring which makes it easy to recognise the difference between fact and fiction. But I would not have thought that *Crime of the Week* would have had this same effect upon its devotees. However, when I

came upon Bertie standing on the doorstep of 221b complete with his box and obviously preparing to depart he
rather made me change this belief by saying, 'Ere, Doctor
Watson, do you think this Ruxton Lake cove would be
likely to need a pageboy?'

The Teacup Mystery

'I've got a little problem of the kind which might appeal to you, Mr Holmes. Of course I will soon have the answer to it, but I thought you might like to exercise that brilliant brain of yours before I arrive at the answer.'

The words were spoken by Inspector George Lestrade with faint touches of sarcasm. We had not seen the man from Scotland Yard for quite a while and I felt that Sherlock Holmes was delighted to see him, though he showed this delight in a manner crab-like. 'I'm always pleased to contribute some small glimmerings of aid, Inspector, however obvious my pronouncements might be. After all, such tiny sparks have often in the past aided to light the tinder box of your mental powers.' Holmes matched the inspector with sarcasm which seemed to pass unnoticed.

Then Lestrade explained his problem. 'An elderly widower, John Watkins, has been discovered dead by a neighbour in the kitchen of his home in Beckenham. His head was slumped forward upon the table. It was assumed at first that he had died of a heart attack but the local police sergeant became suspicious and that is where I was brought in. The sergeant drew my attention to the fragments of a broken teacup which lay under the poor man's forehead and reckoned that simply falling forward onto it might not have shattered it quite so completely.

'When I raised Watkins's head I noticed that one fragment had entered his forehead and it seemed that perhaps his head would need to have been raised up and banged against the table with much force to produce that result. The police surgeon has confirmed that the sliver of china was the principal cause of death. The neighbour seems to be a highly respectable woman and trusted with his key yet there is no other disturbance to suggest a burglar or intruder of any sort.'

Holmes knocked out his pipe upon the upright of the fireplace and then blew through it prior to stretching out a slim hand in the direction of the Turkish slipper. He said, 'Interesting, Inspector. Tell me, is the scene of the tragedy as yet undisturbed?'

Lestrade spoke proudly, 'Yes it is. I left instructions that everything was to remain and everything was to stay as it was until you had seen it.' He said this with the air of a schoolboy who had done his homework.

Holmes nodded approvingly. 'Well, Watson, I think we should go with the inspector to Beckenham without delay. You may have left instructions, Lestrade, but the best-laid plans are not always observed by others.' He did not finish speaking for he was already making ready to depart for Kent.

The horse between the shafts of Lestrade's gig was a good one and kept up a spanking pace all the way to the small Kentish town. I remarked upon the animal being a good one. Holmes replied, 'Of course, it is Lestrade's own gelding.'

The inspector started, 'Did I mention that Dandy was my own horse? I don't remember doing so.'

Holmes replied, 'There was no need, Inspector. I observed the way you glanced admiringly at the animal when
we climbed into the gig. Moreover, I noticed that the
constable driving this equipage has not used his whip,
doubtless following your instructions. Oh yes and I also
note that it does not wear the regulation bit.'

Lestrade grunted. 'Too sharp those bits, I'm not having
his mouth ruined; soft as velvet it is.'

When we arrived at Kent Villa we were ushered into the
kitchen where we were assured by the local sergeant that
nothing had been disturbed apart from the removal of the
body to the police mortuary. The table was covered by a
canvas cloth of the kind which has been enamelled white.
The broken china teacup fragments lay, seemingly where
they had been broken from contact with the head of the
unfortunate Mr Watkins. There was a matching china teapot, a hot-water jug and a sugar bowl.

Holmes stood well back at first, just taking in the complete scene before he neared the table gently touching this
and that with his forefinger tip. Then with finger and
thumb he raised the lid of the teapot and gazed inside.
'Have you made inquiries concerning Mr Watkins of his
neighbours, Sergeant?' But it was Lestrade who answered
as if not wishing to be left out of the conversation.

He said, 'They all agree that he was a bit of a recluse and
extremely careful with his money.'

Holmes nodded, 'Everything around us suggests that, the
modest furnishings, the painted tablecloth which would save
soap and the sparsely filled larder. Yet he used two or more
spoonfuls of tea in a pot meant for one person. The pot is a
small one and there are a great many leaves still inside.'

Lestrade looked interested, 'You mean he had a visitor taking tea with him? There was no one else here when Mrs Johnson discovered him. She seems above reproach, by the way. An elderly lady who looks in now and then to see that he is not sick; he has had a minor heart attack you see.'

Holmes nodded, 'This time it would have taken a more than minor attack to make him slump forward with force enough to shatter the tea cup so. Inspector, do you think you could get me some glue of the kind which is used to mend broken china?'

Lestrade sent his constable to fetch the glue and Holmes turned to me. 'Watson, perhaps you should go to the police mortuary and examine the body?'

I knew better than to ask Holmes why he wanted the glue or to argue other small points. So, as soon as Lestrade's constable driver returned with the glue, Lestrade and I set out for that gruesome institution where bodies are stored.

The cadaver which had been John Watkins was laid still upon the examination slab and I could see the terrible wound upon his forehead where the sliver of china had evidently pierced not only the flesh but the skull. The police surgeon showed us the piece of teacup involved, now safely isolated in a small bag.

Lestrade suggested that he should take charge of this piece of evidence. The surgeon was not delighted when Lestrade suggested that I be allowed to make an examination of the late Mr Watkins but he shrugged his permission.

I wasted little time upon the forehead wound, feeling that this was undoubtedly where the cause of death could be found. I looked for the signs of a recent heart seizure and finding none I started a wider examination, eventually finding two symmetrical bruises, one on each side of the neck at the back. I felt that these could have been consistent with his head having been forcefully thrust down, perhaps a number of times.

We returned to Beckenham and Lestrade seemed quite pleased with the pronouncements that I made as the gig took us there. 'An open-and-shut case of murder by a person unknown.'

As we entered Kent Villa, I went straight through to the kitchen where, to my amazement, Holmes was putting the finishing touches to the reconstruction of the shattered teacup. The restored utensil stood there, seemingly complete save for one fairly large piece at the rim. Lestrade took in what Holmes had been doing without immediate comment. Then he looked thoughtful, took the enclosed china fragment in its packet from his pocket and offered it to Holmes. 'The last piece for your restoration?' Holmes took the piece from its packet and slotted it into place.

Lestrade grinned and said, 'Waste of time and glue. What does it prove?'

Holmes took an envelope from his pocket and poured forth from it perhaps half a dozen small china fragments saying, 'Here are a few that simply will not fit the reconstruction. You see, Inspector, there were two teacups broken, but whoever was taking tea with Watkins evidently killed him and then tried to remove the fragments of the second cup. I suspected the involvement of another tea imbiber from the amount of leaves in the pot.'

I told Holmes of my findings at the mortuary, concerning the bruises at the neck of the body. He said, 'Good work, Watson, the pattern begins to emerge. Watkins had a visitor taking tea with him, someone he trusted or at least had no fear of. The sugar bowl is empty so possibly the murderer crossed to that Welsh dresser at the wall behind where Watkins sat. There is a sugar bowl there also. To fetch more sugar could have been the excuse the person unknown needed to grasp Watkins by the neck at the rear and smash his head repeatedly forward onto the table. The teacups got in the way so the murderer swept up the pieces of the second cup but managed to overlook a few of them, or more likely thought they were part of the cup which lay shattered beneath Watkins's head.'

Lestrade did not argue with Holmes's pronouncements. 'I suppose Mrs Johnson is out of the question for she appears to have no motive and indeed seems to have gone out of her way to be kind to the otherwise neglected man.'

Holmes surprised me by replying, 'Oh, I don't know, Inspector, stranger things have happened.' As we walked up the path leading to the nearby house where Mrs Johnson lived my friend lagged behind a little. He said, 'Inspector, you are known to the lady and will not disturb or distress her and Watson is a medical man. I think it would be better that the two of you go in first and give her warning that a third person in the persona of myself will be visiting her. Come, I will follow in a few moments.'

Lestrade grinned at me as he pulled the door bell. 'Sherlock is getting very considerate in his old age, Doctor.' I nodded curtly, suspecting some ulterior motive concerned with Holmes's dalliance. As for old Mrs Johnson, she was quite tearful still, evidently much saddened by the passing of her neighbour. She said, 'Poor gentleman, he was such a lonely soul; still, he is at peace now.'

Lestrade told her of the impending visit of the world's most famous detective, although he did not use those actual words, saying, 'There's a friend of mine, interested in police work but quite a tiro, coming too. He is Mr Sherlock Holmes and he will be here any minute.'

I fancied, just fancied, that a steely glint came into Mrs Johnson's eyes at the mention of my friend's name but when Holmes himself presented himself she was all smiles, if tearful ones, greeting Holmes like an old friend. 'Mr Holmes, how nice to meet you in person after reading of your exploits in the *Strand* but I do wish it was under happier circumstances.'

She busied herself with making us a pot of tea and whilst she could be heard pottering in the kitchen Holmes produced from beneath his coat a paper bag which he showed to contain some china fragments matching those found on Watkins's table. 'I took the opportunity to rummage in the dustbin. I had a feeling that I would find these. Now all you need is a motive, Inspector.'

I had been idly leafing though the pages of a photograph album which stood upon an occasional table. My eyes lit upon a photograph of a stiffly posed group. Two of the persons I seemed to recognise. I said, 'Well I don't know the motive, but I can see that Mrs Johnson knew Mr Watkins — at least many years ago she did.'

Holmes studied the picture, muttered, 'Well done, my dear fellow; only you of the two of us could recognise Watkins but you have only seen him dead. Can you be sure?' I nodded, and as sounds from the kitchen suggested the impending return of Mrs Johnson I hastily returned the album to its place.

Lestrade aided the lady to set down the tray she bore and asked her, 'Mrs Johnson, I believe that you only moved into this district recently and had not known Mr Watkins previously?'

She said, 'That is correct, Inspector. I had not been here long when I realised that poor old John was practically blind and needed someone to look in on him two or three times a day, which I did.'

Lestrade asked, 'When you discovered the poor man slumped over the table did you get the impression that he had been entertaining anyone for tea?'

She said, with a touch of over-confidence it was to turn out, 'No, I noticed that there was only one cup on the table.' Then she looked a little furtive and said, 'Funny how you can notice something like that, isn't it, at such a dramatic moment?'

Holmes said, 'Mrs Johnson, is it not true that you swept up the pieces of the second cup in order that it would not be noticed?'

She looked aghast, 'Why would I do a thing like that?'

My friend said, 'It is as logical as is your moving to a house near a man you had known well and who was blind enough not to recognise you; to worm your way into his confidence and then murder him.'

The production of the china fragments and the turning of the album to the picture and Holmes's other findings were enough to produce an outburst of confession, 'He ruined my sister; married her and ill-used her until she died years before her time. Of course I moved into this house and planned the whole thing. Well, I was unlucky . . .'

Lestrade said, 'Mrs Ivy Johnson, I arrest you for the murder of one John Watkins . . .'

She interrupted, 'You would never have found me out, Inspector. You had to bring Sherlock Holmes onto the scene to do it. That is what I mean by unlucky.'

The Maestro's Problem

'How do you fancy a musical evening, Watson?' I was staying with my friend Sherlock Holmes at our old rooms in Baker Street for a few days. I had been spared his violin playing for long enough to imagine that for this specific visit I was going to escape this particular aspect of Holmes's activities. The reader should not misunderstand my words; Holmes is an accomplished musician and I am not completely without an interest in music. No, it is rather his choice of pieces that baffles me and sometimes brings on an earache, from which I have suffered ever since I found myself too close to the artillery in Afghanistan.

Mozart, Schubert, even Strauss I can listen to with pleasure; but my friend seems to discover pieces for the violin which are enigmatic to say the least. Often I have suspected that he is not only the composer himself but actually in the composing process at the time of his playing! But I have ever been the diplomat concerning such things, so I replied, 'Ah, so you are going to play something, what?'

Holmes chuckled as he said, 'Good old Watson, really you should be a politician, but no, I had no plans to assault your ears with my own efforts. It is just that my friend Concelli is giving a concert at the Carstairs Hall. He has sent me two tickets, so would you care to accompany me?'

Vastly relieved yet anxious not to appear so I said, 'Why yes, Holmes, I would be delighted but please do not remain under the misapprehension that I do not appreciate your own musical talents.'

Mercifully Holmes became involved in the organisation of our concert-going expedition. He set Billy to smoothing his silk hat with a velvet pad and Mrs Hudson to ironing his dress coat. Fortunately I had brought my own formal wear from my home.

As we travelled that evening to Carstairs Hall, which was south of the Thames quite close to where Astleys had been, Holmes said, 'I have known Signor Concelli for many years, Watson, since I was able to be of service to him in Florence when I was able to recover a lost manuscript for him. I do not believe you were with me on that occasion but I feel sure I have mentioned the episode to you.'

I nodded, 'Yes, and of course he is known to me by his international fame as a composer and conductor.'

He said, 'He is no mere conductor, my dear fellow, for he is also a great showman. I think you will enjoy some of his fireworks!'

A large audience had assembled to hear Concelli's music and to watch his dynamic style of conducting. After the gentlemen of the orchestra had entered, the enigmatic-looking Italian took up his position. He was tall and dark with homely enough features save for his huge and seemingly sparkling eyes. I remarked upon his sparkling optics to Holmes who said, 'It is amazing what Bella Donna will do, Watson.' Then his right index finger went up to his lips as the famous musician raised his baton.

The first piece, a lively overture, had that excitement required to awaken the audience's ability to enjoy and certainly it did just that. It was followed by a waltz, as strong as anything by Strauss, yet with a distinctly Italian touch. It was an engaging repertoire on the whole for me, until he began a piece which seemed not just foreign to my ears in the geographical sense but unlike anything I had ever heard. Oriental? No, not quite, but exotic and bizarre are words that spring to my mind. Holmes obviously enjoyed what he heard and leant forward in his seat.

Yet suddenly I realised that it was not just rapt attention to the music which caused the stiffening of Holmes's sinews. He nudged me and pointed to draw my attention to a flautist who had risen from his seat and was holding his flute to his lips as one might expect, yet at a rather unusual and impractical angle. Holmes muttered, 'A special solo I wonder?' But soon we both realised this was not so from the reaction of Concelli who had stopped conducting the orchestra and was staring at the flautist in amazement.

Then suddenly the dramatic situation came to a climax which brought the dwindling notes from the orchestra to a complete stop. The flautist swayed upon his feet, dropped the flute, then slowly collapsed amid falling music stands.

Concelli was well up to facing an emergency and his clear voice carried through the hall, 'Ladies and gentlemen, please there is an emergency but not to worry you, eh? First may I ask, is there a doctor in the hall?' Naturally I felt bound to make myself known, which I did, leaping to my feet and making for the platform, closely followed by Sherlock Holmes.

My first action was to push my way through the musical

instruments and their owners, quite aside from a sea of music stands. But I eventually reached the still figure of the fallen flautist. He had dropped suddenly like a stone and lay inert. I could see that the fellow was dead but I went through the ritual of feeling for a pulse and touching his neck. Holmes had already sent for the police but stood guard over the body meanwhile, keeping others at their distance. He said, 'Only Doctor Watson should touch the poor fellow until the police and ambulance men arrive.' Then more quietly he enquired of me, 'Watson, I take it that life is extinct?'

I said, 'Very much so, he appears to have been felled by a heart seizure or stroke.'

Holmes, however, doubted my words, 'Look at the blue tinge of his complexion.'

I asked, 'You mean he could have been poisoned?'

He replied, 'It is possible, but I suppose we must wait for the police surgeon to be sure. Meanwhile let us find out what we can before Scotland Yard interfere with all chances of investigation.'

Holmes turned to the flautist in the seat next to the deceased, 'You knew this poor fellow?'

The flautist shook his head. 'Should have been Jeremy Clark. In fact, Jeremy was waiting in the dressing room with the rest of us before the concert and just before the signal for us to make an entrance.' Enquiry among other musicians confirmed that Mr Clark must have been the last man to leave the dressing room.

Another flautist confirmed that the dead man had been the last to be seated, saying, 'I knew that Jeremy was late, I thought this fellow was a deputy when he took his seat.'

Holmes leapt into action, 'Watch the body until the police get here, Watson. I must look for Mr Jeremy Clark.'

I did what I could to keep things organised but having my work cut out to calm the excited conductor and to prevent any interference with the scene itself. Within about a further five minutes the police arrived in the shape of two constables and a Detective Sergeant Fowler. The latter proved to be a regular bulldog of a young man, anxious to get as much detail of the incident as he could in the shortest possible time.

I introduced myself and told him that Holmes had gone to the dressing room in search of the flautist. I conveyed as much as I could of what we had learned. He was grateful that we had left everything as undisturbed as possible. 'I know all about Sherlock Holmes of course and his theories. The old boys at the Yard think he is the cat's whiskers.'

When Sherlock Holmes reappeared on the scene he had with him a small man, sparse of locks and wearing a dressing gown. He introduced him. 'Mr Jeremy Clark, flautist, the man who should have been sitting where the dead man sat. He was attacked from behind as he started for the door and overcome, before he could even speak, by a small dark man wearing shabby clothes who bound and gagged him.'

Mr Clark nodded glumly, 'Then he took my clothes and left me bound and helplessly gagged, which is the state in which Mr Holmes found me. What did he have against me, I'd like to know? Why, I've never set eyes on him before.'

Holmes said, 'Whichever flautist had been the last to leave the room would have been his victim, he just wanted to change places with one of you.'

Clark gasped, 'But why?'

Concelli threw up his hands and also asked, 'Why Sherlock, my friend, did this little brown fellow do this and why is he dead?'

The detective sergeant laid a reassuring hand on the conductor's shoulder. 'Never mind all that, sir, leave it to us.' Concelli caught Holmes's eye and gave a magnificent Italian shrug.

Holmes said, 'Of course, Sergeant, but if I can help I will be happy to do so.'

The Yard man looked at Holmes and spoke in a rather patronising manner. 'Oh, of course, the great Sherlock Holmes will probably solve this little mystery in a few minutes.' As he spoke the ambulance men took away the body of the small dark man and the two constables started to try to justify their existence by searching the area surrounding the dead flautist's chair and taking statements from his immediate neighbours.

Holmes said, 'Of course the police have much to do in order to establish the identity of the dead man, the cause of his death and his reason for wanting to take the place of the official musician. Signor Concelli, what was the title of that piece that you were playing when this bizarre incident occurred?'

Concelli said, 'It was my new piece, based upon a native Brazilian folk tune; known only to the Indians until I heard it on my travels in that vast country.'

Holmes nodded, 'Is it coincidence that the dead man was a Brazilian Indian do you think?'

The sergeant started, 'How do you know that?'

Holmes said, 'From my studies of ethnic groups; you

should read my monograph upon the subject. The fellow had the right appearance to fill that role. Also around his neck an artefact that made his origin near obvious. He hid in the dressing room on the chance that he could take the steps that he took.'

The sergeant looked at Holmes with doubt in his solid face. 'But why?'

Holmes smiled, 'To kill Signor Concelli, I imagine. You see he might have been the composer of the melody upon which Concelli has based his new composition, doubtless under the impression that the tune was traditional.'

Concelli nodded, 'That is what I believed. I would not steal another's work!'

Fowler almost shrieked, 'But good Lord, man, we are investigating the death of the Indian himself!'

Holmes nodded, 'That is so as it has fallen out, but his own death is an accident, Concelli was indeed his intended victim.'

The sergeant said, 'Mr Holmes, sir, with all due respect, I think your theory is very much short of complete. How was he going to kill Concelli and why did he die himself instead?'

Holmes picked up the discarded musical instrument and asked, 'May I look at this, and see if it will advance my theory?'

Sergeant Fowler laughed, 'His flute is not going to tell us much!'

My friend agreed, 'No, Jeremy Clark's flute will not tell us much because it never left the dressing room. This is not actually a flute, simply a bamboo tube which has been decorated to look like one. Observe, Watson, even the holes are false, being just black painted dots.' I examined that which I had never doubted to be a flute.

I said, 'Good Lord, Holmes, you mean this is a native pipe for the expulsion of poisoned darts?'

Sherlock said, 'That is my belief.'

There was a silence lasting perhaps ten seconds, then Fowler said, 'I see, but Concelli is still on his feet, and the Indian is dead. What happened, did he miss the target with his dart and die of a heart attack from the shock?' He was ladling the sarcasm treacle thick now.

I confess that I too could not quite see how the Holmes theory tied in with what had occurred. I said, 'Holmes, there is a point there.'

My friend replied, with an acidic tone, 'Watson, Fowler, can you not see what happened? The Indian, having changed into the flautist's suit, left him trussed up in the dressing room and then came onto the platform, holding the pipe disguised as a flute. The other musicians assumed that he was a last-minute replacement. Whilst they possibly wondered why he did not play they could scarcely interrupt less they catch the sharp edge of Concelli tongue. Then, when the actual disputed piece commenced, he raised the blow-pipe. No one tried to prevent him, thinking he was scheduled for a flute solo! Unfortunately for him, in attempting to expel the deadly little dart at the conductor, he breathed in at the wrong moment and swallowed the missile. The blue tinge of his skin and contortion of his features told me this. So there, my dear Fowler, is the theory in its entirety. Your surgeon will doubtless confirm what I have said.'

We had to wait for this confirmation of Holmes's theory until the morrow, but meanwhile Concelli insisted on taking us to dinner at his hotel. As we demolished, between us, an excellent bottle of Beaujolais, Holmes said, 'My dear Signor Concelli, in order to avoid any repetition of this grisly business, dare I suggest that you summon the newspapers and ask them to publicise the fact that your piece is based upon the work of a native Brazilian. Moreover, another suggestion for what it is worth; hold a special concert and play the piece as a feature, giving a goodly percentage to the Brazilian Indians.'

Back at Baker Street I was all but ready for my bed when Holmes suddenly loosened his dress cravat and picked up his violin. He put it to his chin and started to tinker upon it. Then he lowered his bow and said to me, 'Watson, I will play only one short piece. Oh, and try to consider how fortunate you are that I do not play the flute.'

The Baker Street Conjurer

Until comparatively recent times there was a hostelry in Baker Street called the Cold Cut and Tankard. Its eye-catching inn sign, depicting a mouth-watering ham beside a tall tankard of ale, attracting more than a fair share of the passing trade as well as countless regular patrons. Holmes and I were wont to drop in to that public house for a portion of cheddar and a modest pint of beer. The fact that there was ever a crowd in the place seemed to endear it to the world's most celebrated investigator. 'All human life is here, Watson, from dukes to dustmen!'

The proprietor of this house, or perhaps I should in more popular style refer to him as the publican, was a large hearty man, George Dean, extremely popular with his regular clientele. George kept an extremely orderly house with seldom any bar-room brawls to disturb one's quiet consumption of a drink and a bite.

Usually he was as hearty of manner as his appearance would suggest; yet I recollect an occasion when we found him strangely thoughtful and quiet. I remarked upon this, asking, 'Mr Dean, you look as if you have lost a shilling and found a threepenny piece. Come sir, what ails the good landlord?'

George Dean sighed and answered, 'Funny that you

should say that, Doctor, for it is not far from the truth. As you know I employ only members of my own family as far as access to the tills is concerned. They are all — my daughters and my wife and my son-in-law — completely trustworthy, yet, Doctor, I have of late been consistently light on one of my tills, always by the same amount and at very regular intervals.

'There is a pattern in it and I have my suspicions regarding the culprit who is among my regulars. I can make no accusation without making myself foolish on account of complete lack of proof. Moreover the person concerned is an agreeable fellow, very popular with my clientele. How he can be connected with it is beyond me, yet it always happens on those days when he is here.'

I said, 'George, this sounds like a problem that my friend Sherlock Holmes should hear about.' Although George seemed loath to trouble my friend, I called Holmes over to the quiet corner of the bar where we stood. Dean repeated his tale of woe and Holmes, whilst he showed no great interest, would not refuse to consider the publican's problem.

He asked, 'Landlord, what sort is this man who is popular with your regulars yet who seems always, perhaps by coincidence, to be present whenever your till has a shortage?'

Dean said, 'Well, Mr Holmes, he is a smart-looking man, in his thirties, who comes in here just about every other day accompanied by two or three friends. He stands at the bar and whilst partaking of his pint he indulges in a series of amazing conjuring tricks. He asks nothing in return and I feel sure that many patrons are attracted here by his performances.'

Holmes asked, 'Cutting all the corners, can you describe a typical soirée with the fellow?'

The landlord began a fairly lengthy narration. 'Well, sir, it usually starts when he has bought a round of drinks and I am giving him his change from a sovereign. He cups his right hand and I drop the coins into it. He closes the hand, opens it again to show that all the coins have gone, vanished, disappeared! Then he will buy a meat pie and cut it open to reveal a half-crown inside it. He always takes it out and remarks "Good value these pies, George!" Then he will call for a pack of cards and will perform some amazing feats with them always managing to produce the chosen card no matter how difficult the conditions may be made for him.

'But his final trick is invariably that in which he borrows from me a five-pound note. He has me make note of the number and even sign my name upon it. He causes the note to disappear and then causes it to reappear in one of the other tills. I don't know how he does it, and I don't know for certain that the shortcomings in the takings is even connected with his presence, so I have not said anything to him on the subject. After all, if I do he might take offence and my patrons look forward to his little performances but four pounds, ten shillings is a loss worthy of consideration. Always it is the same amount.'

Holmes purchased a half corona from George and lit it thoughtfully. At last he spoke, asking, 'Is the mysterious five-pound note always found in the same till?'

Dean said, 'Why no, it sometimes reappears in the till in the public bar, or sometimes the one in the snug.'

My friend asked, 'Is the shortage always from the till in which it reappears?'

George answered, 'Yes sir, it is.'

I could tell that Sherlock Holmes was now well and truly intrigued by the mystery of the vanishing fiver and the disappearing takings.

He asked, 'When do you estimate that your conjuring friend will next make an appearance? I feel that if I witnessed his performance I might get some idea as to a possible connection between his conjurations and your losses.'

It transpired that the landlord was reasonably certain that his mysterious patron would be in the private bar that very evening at about seven of the clock, saying, 'That is if he follows the pattern of recent weeks, Mr Holmes.'

So it was then that we found ourselves comfortably seated at seven that evening, awaiting the arrival of the conjurer. We spotted our quarry, recognising him from the landlord's description and from the jaunty way he made an entrance; there was something all but theatrical in the way he did it. I could see at once how loath George would be to accuse such an open-looking and friendly-seeming individual as having any connection with wrongdoing.

We watched, fascinated, as he caused a chosen playing card to leap out of the pack and produced real half-crowns from the ears, noses and headgear of the interested spectators. A little shabbily-dressed bystander demanded, 'Show us the one with the fiver, guv'nor!' Some of the regulars joining in the demand. The conjurer shrugged and allowed himself to be talked into it. He appealed for the loan of a five-pound note, glancing at George Dean insinuatingly. George hesitated, caught Holmes's eye, and took a five-pound note from his till. As if by habit he scribbled its number upon a scrap of paper which he placed beside the till.

The conjurer took the banknote and folded it into a small compass. He draped a handkerchief over the folded note and asked several people around him in turn to peer under this drape to assure themselves that it was there. Then suddenly he threw the cambric square into the air: the banknote had vanished. There were gasps of astonishment despite the obvious fact that many of the patrons had seen him do it before. But there was a diversion at this point as the plausible one produced a shower of monkey nuts from the handkerchief. But at last he smiled wryly at George and said, 'Mine host, your five-pound note is safely in the till in your snug bar. Please be kind enough to find it and check that its number is correct.'

There was a general babble of congratulatory noises from the patrons as George Dean checked the numbers on the banknote against those upon his scrap of paper. The conjurer finished his drink and bade an effusive farewell to the company in general. Holmes turned to me and said, 'Follow him, Watson. Be discreet, and try to find out if he visits any other hostelries in the area and if they too have till shortages.'

I shadowed the fellow along Baker Street and into the Marylebone Road. I noted with interest that he walked alone and not in company with anyone from the Cold Cut and Tankard. However, he entered a public house called The Horse and Hounds and, lurking in the shadows, I saw him repeat the performance that he had given earlier with just minor variation. From there I followed him to the King's Cross Hotel, which he entered in company with a small man whom he had greeted outside the building. Once inside he gave a third performance.

At the first of these two places I had no chance to enquire regarding till shortages because I had not wanted to lose my quarry, however after he left the bar at King's Cross I decided to risk losing him. I hung around and got into conversation with a barmaid with extremely golden hair and ample bosom. I led the conversation very gently toward possible lost takings. When I finally did touch on the subject her manner changed and she became defensive. 'Ow did you know about the missing four pounds ten bob. Are you from the head office or something?' I tipped my hat and left, having gained the information I wanted.

Back at 221b I was to learn from Holmes that George Dean had indeed found his snug bar till to be four pounds ten shillings short. I told him of my adventures and that our quarry had appeared to enter each hostelry with a different companion. I also told him that at least one other bar had suffered from a four pounds ten shilling shortfall. He grunted, 'Of course, he uses confederates but is smart enough to use a different one at each scene of operation. Doubtless he shuffles them about to further put anyone off the scent. I saw the man with him at the Cold Cut and Tankard for what he was.'

I was puzzled. 'What makes you say that? He looked like a rather scruffy individual, not at all well dressed like the suspect.'

Holmes smiled enigmatically, 'You noticed his shabby jacket and his seedy trousers but what else?' I couldn't think that there had been anything else about him to take particular note of and said as much. My friend said, 'Watson, the man was wearing a pair of boots that had been made especially for him at a cost of perhaps ten guineas at St James.'

I asked, 'How can you say that they were made to measure or that they were not given to him by a wealthy benefactor?'

Holmes chuckled, 'As often occurs, one of his feet was rather larger than the other, yet the shoes, which were of excellent quality, fitted both feet perfectly.

'According to George Dean our quarry will be at the Cold Cut and Tankard on the evening after next. We will be there and I have a part that you must play, Watson.' During the next few minutes he explained what I would be required to do. 'We will stand near the bar, and close to our suspects. Then at a moment when I give you the nudge you will as quietly as possible direct the small man away from the scene. Then, when you have got him to a suitable distance you will use your ingenuity to hold his attention for a few minutes; I leave the means to your inventiveness.'

Some forty hours later we were in George Dean's Saloon Bar and Holmes was seemingly as calm as ever but I confess that I was in a state of excitement and anxiety at the thought of what I had to engage myself with. Soon after seven of the clock the man who we had grown to refer to as the conjurer entered, and I noticed that the scruffy little man with the expensive shoes was not far behind him.

The events took an almost identical turn to those of our previous experience of the deft-fingered trickster's exhibition, except that some of the card tricks were different. Then, when he was well involved with the landlord's five-pound note, Holmes poked a boney finger into my ribs and I turned to face the small man and started to push him firmly but gently toward the door. He started to protest but I put a finger to my lips and smiled enigmatically as if to infer that my actions were leading to some advantage to himself. He was puzzled but after a while he started to try and push past me. Then it was that I had to use force which he resisted, forcing me to drop him with a right hook to the jaw. The incredible thing was that I had managed all this without causing any great noise or general disturbance. The little fellow rose to his feet and after one or two aggressive movements in my direction thought better of it and made his escape through the main door of the tavern and scuttled down Baker Street.

I eased my way back to where Holmes was standing, to find that an argument had broken out between the publican and the conjurer. The disagreement centred around the fact the trickster had claimed that the vanished five-pound note would be found in the public bar till. When it had failed to materialise there George had caused all of the taverns tills to be searched, but no banknote of that denomination was present — all similarity of numbering aside.

It was hardly surprising that Dean demanded recompense for his elusive fiver. With a very long face the conjurer took a five-pound note from his wallet and handed it to George, saying, 'No offence, guv'nor, accidents will happen. I'll see you again soon, when the spirits are more willing, so to speak.'

At this point Holmes introduced himself to the conjurer by presenting his card and saying, 'I feel, sir, that it would be to your advantage to confine your legerdemain to some other district for the foreseeable future.'

It was not until the clock over the saloon bar had struck ten and the last of the stragglers had obeyed George's stentorian utterances of 'Time, gentlemen, please' that Holmes was able to explain to George and me just exactly what had happened.

'My dear Dean, you had been the regular victim of a confidence trick new even to my not inconsiderable experience of such things. You see at a moment when everyone was convinced that your folded five-pound note was still in the handkerchief it was actually in the left palm of the trickster. He passed it to the small man who stood close beside him whilst directing all attention to the handkerchief. He continued to hold that interest, giving the shifty one a chance to slip away to one of the other bars where he would spend ten shillings upon drinks and take four pounds ten shillings in change. Dean's five-pound note could then be identified as if it had floated to that till by magic.'

I think it clear to say that both Dean and I had followed that which Holmes had explained, clearly enough. But it was George who was the more puzzled than I concerning the events of that evening. He asked, 'Why then did the trick not work this time?'

Holmes chuckled, 'Watson, on my instructions, waylaid the confederate. It was my hand which took the note from the conjurer and even he did not realise that his friend was not he who took it.' My friend took out his wallet and extracted from it a folded five-pound note which he unfurled and handed to the now genial landlord.

He said, 'Mr Holmes, you are a wonder! How you twigged

it, I can't imagine. I've got a tenner toward my losses, and the rest I am happy to write down to experience. I will not be taken in by that trick again!'

Holmes waited until we had left the building and were walking along Baker Street before saying, 'I wonder, Watson what other confidence tricks he will fall for? We really must keep an eye on friend Dean!'